Stone the Goat

Stone the Goat

by

Mary Walley Kalbert

Dream Lake Publishing
Friday Harbor, WA

All rights reserved. No part of this book may be reproduced in any manner whatsoever without written permission of the publisher.

Stone the Goat
Copyright © 2018 by Mary Walley Kalbert

Dream Lake Publishing
Friday Harbor, Washington

Book design by Pam Herber
Author photograph by Pam Herber

Library of Congress Control Number: 2017916032

ISBN: 978-0-9824282-4-5

Text set in Adobe Garamond Pro

First Edition

To my mothers

Mary Maud Smith Walley
and
Nola Meadows Walley

whose lives, before they were wives,
should be remembered, too

Contents

Chapter One	1
Chapter Two	11
Chapter Three	21
Chapter Four	39
Chapter Five	53
Chapter Six	69
Chapter Seven	81
Chapter Eight	103
Chapter Nine	119
Chapter Ten	135
Chapter Eleven	143
Chapter Twelve	157
Chapter Thirteen	173
Chapter Fourteen	187
Chapter Fifteen	209
Chapter Sixteen	223
Chapter Seventeen	237

Note from the Author

This book is a work of fiction that has been twelve years in the making. It is my first foray into fiction.

There is a two-fold purpose to this book. The first is to provide a glimpse of another culture through the eyes of an American woman with enough conflict and action to please readers. The second is to prove to myself I could accomplish this. The second purpose has been as difficult as the first.

The short amount of time I spent in Turkey was augmented by many hours of research, some for information, some for the sheer pleasure of reading about the country and its people.

To further the story, great liberties have been taken with the geography of the Taurus mountains and surrounding areas as well as the culture of the nomadic tribes of Turkey.

I created a tribe whose sole purpose is to propel my protagonist as she steams and stumbles her way through turmoil and danger. The name given to the tribe is Saz, specifically because it is a word which easily rolls off the tongue. It is the Turkish word for a stringed musical instrument.

All the characters are fictitious. Two have been imbued with the character traits of people I admire.

All errors are mine.

This book has been written using the tools found in *Writing the Breakout Novel* by Donald Maass.

It is my sincere hope that when one finishes this book there will be a scene or a bit of dialogue that will linger long after the last page has been read.

Here are a few words and their meanings:

şerefe	Cheers!
şalvar	voluminous trousers worn by women and men
şamovar	urn to make tea
yufka	a thin sheet of dough that makes a bread that can last six months
yayla	high plateau in the mountains

Stone the Goat

Chapter One

April 1st 1989

YOU DON'T HAVE *to do this. Mr. Beyter would understand. Not all promises can be kept.*

Maggie Meadows stood near the French windows of her hotel room as a breeze from the Mediterranean Sea danced with the sheer curtain. She picked up the heavy envelope that lay on the rumpled bed, rubbed the embossed name with her thumb and lifted it to her nose to catch the lingering scent of tobacco.

Maggie looked out over the ancient harbor in old part of the city of Antalya. It was wrapped in a cloak of lingering twilight. Old fishing boats creaked in protest against their moorings, their cabins warmed by golden squares of light that filled the windows.

Slowly she withdrew the letter and unfolded it for the second time.

Dearest Maggie,
When you read this letter, you will have attended my funeral and reflected on our years of working together. Now you must

continue our work alone. I know you can.

I chose you those years ago, from all the applicants for my scholarship programs, because of the life you had lived. You wrote of the hardscrabble life of your nomadic childhood. You asked for an opportunity to leave that life through education. I looked for self-pity in your essay, and found none.

I was searching for someone who had endured enough to know what hardship was, someone who could live in a different culture and participate as an equal in the difficulties they would have to endure. I found that in you.

I commit to paper what we agreed upon earlier when I realized my health would not permit me to continue my work. Now is the time for you to go and work in the Taurus Mountains for a season with the women of my tribe. The women will listen to you, Maggie, because you can share and understand the harshness of their lives.

Convince the women to continue weaving their carpets as they have for a thousand years. Use your knowledge and my Foundation to show them foreigners can learn, appreciate, and help them preserve our ways. They are the keepers of our heritage. If the women stop weaving our history, it will die.

Maggie stopped reading. Mr. Beyter had always believed in her, long before the time she had believed in herself. She folded the letter and carefully placed it back into the envelope.

With a glance at the bedside clock she scuffed her way to the bathroom. Clouds of steam rose as water followed soap around the curves, splashed down the hollows and streamed into the crevices of her body. Minutes later she stood damp and naked on the warm tile floor and swiped the foggy mirror with her arm. Her eyes traveled down to a single breast. She stifled an involuntary sigh.

One more reason not to go.

She picked up a prosthetic breast and slid it into the left pocket of her mastectomy bra; slipped the bra on; then snapped, tugged, swiveled; surveyed the alignment; and then shifted and tugged again. She critiqued the alignment once more.

Voices from the cobblestone street below floated upward. Maggie fastened her dress and stepped onto the balcony to see a young couple sauntering by, illuminated by a soft pool of light from the hotel entrance.

Maggie returned a wave to Omar, the carpet merchant, whose small shop adjoined the hotel. He was moving his postcard stands into his shop. Tomorrow he would bring them out again to entice tourists inside to browse and buy.

Maggie breathed in a long breath of the moist air and drew the French windows together. She tucked the letter into a small handbag and made her way down the marble steps to the elegant lobby of the old hotel. Her normally upturned lips disciplined themselves for the sparring ahead.

Maggie entered the lounge and the pianist nodded in her direction. She angled her way to a table and a low curved sofa in the far corner. The full-length window provided a view to the outdoor area of the restaurant where comfortable chairs were placed near scattered tables in front of the turquoise swimming pool.

The Residence Hotel had been Maggie's home for the four years she had worked on business projects in the southern part of Turkey. Her employer, Mr. Mustafa Beyter, recently deceased, had offered her lodging at any of the luxury hotels along the beach or the use of a private apartment. Here, in Kaleiçi, Antalya's old town—with narrow streets and long-time merchants hawking their wares, street sweepers she knew by name, and a small bay that reflected the moods of the Mediterranean—this was where she wanted to be.

A young waiter appeared. "A glass of wine, today, would you like?"

"Not today, but thank you," Maggie said. She would have time to help him with his word order later. All the younger wait staff came to Maggie for help with their English.

"Will Haluk be joining you?"

"Yes, eventually," Maggie said. Maybe Haluk hadn't found a guide. Without a guide there would be no trip with the nomads to the mountains. One could pray.

Moments later the pianist twittered and missed a note as Maggie's dinner partner stepped into the restaurant. Haluk, a Georgetown educated Turk with definite Western tendencies owned nine auto dealerships around the country. He spoke eight languages fluently and had been punctual three times in the seven years she had known him. His mass of tawny hair, a compromise of his Norwegian mother and Turkish father, fell thick and tousled to the collar of his Italian suit. He looked down and stopped to pick some microscopic lint from his sleeve.

"Hi." Haluk leaned to kiss her cheek and slid into the chair beside her. "Now I can give you my full attention."

"Hey yourself," Maggie tapped her watch. "You're early, thought I'd have time to read a book while I waited."

"You're terrible." He eyed her blue linen dress, tan heels and gold bangles. "But, you are the most attractive woman in the room."

"I'm the only woman in the room." Maggie looked around.

"There's the pianist." Haluk waved in the direction of the piano and caught her eye. He flashed a brilliant smile across the room, causing her to once again skip a note.

Haluk settled into the chair. He signaled one of the waiters to the table. "I'll have *raki* and Maggie Hanim will have white wine."

"No, I'll have raki as well," Maggie countered.

Haluk's eyes narrowed. "You've only drunk raki once in all the years I've known you."

"Twice," Maggie counted on her fingers, "Once when we came screaming down here from Eskeşehir so you could go to a camel race, and once after you let me fall off a camel in Urfa."

"You barely hurt yourself. Maybe you should stay away from camels. Think of all the things we've done that turned out okay." Haluk stopped talking as a man stepped into the outdoor pool. A woman slithered, with barely a ripple, into the pool beside the man. "We could have some fun if you would stay in Antalya." Haluk's eyes never left the antics of the couple in the turquoise water.

Maggie ignored him. There were pressing matters on her mind. The raki arrived. Haluk added just enough water to his to turn the clear liquor milky. Maggie added water to hers as well, then sipped, shuddered and added more water to the strong anise seed flavored drink. She had never enjoyed it, but there were times when one did what one must, and today a strong drink was a must.

"Did you find me a guide?" Maggie asked.

"Yes, but I haven't hired him," he said.

"Why?" Maggie asked.

"Because you're making a big mistake," Haluk studied the tablecloth intently.

"Don't go to the *yayla*. It's no place for a woman like you. I promised Mr. Beyter I would watch over you, and I can't do that if you are in some nomad tent village so far up in the mountains I can't get to you, and two," he rushed to finish, "I don't want you to leave."

The admission about her took Maggie by surprise. But Haluk's desires weren't important any more. What was true was that the the summer grazing grounds for nomadic tribes high in the Taurus Mountains was difficult to get to.

Maggie slid the letter out of her purse and gently waved it in front of him. "I told Mr. Beyter when I saw him last," Maggie's eyes rested on his, "that I would do everything I could to preserve the traditional carpet making in the tribes." She placed the letter on the table. "Just didn't expect it to be so soon."

"Shouldn't you think about your health?" Haluk glanced

at Maggie's chest. "I don't think he really expected you to go there alone."

"I won't be if you get me a guide," Maggie said. "I'm perfectly fine. I promised him this, face to face. It's as simple as that."

The corner of Haluk's right eye twitched. "You're right. But you should consider *not* doing this." He raised his hand to stop her protest. "Let me finish. This project—mountains, nomads, goats, sheep, camels, and the trip alone to the upper plateaus—will be unlike anything you have ever experienced." A furrow deepened over his eyes. "You could do everything Mr. Beyter asked by living in any of the villages, and I could still get to you."

Maggie leaned forward. "I know enough to know I can't be trusted until I can prove I know what I'm talking about, and that can't be done living in a village. I have to go to the yayla."

"I hope it's not your bones I could be finding all down the mountain if you do this," Haluk shot back.

Maggie drained her glass and set it down carefully. "That makes me feel better already—listen, Haluk, I'm scared to death about this and if you tell anyone that I'll swear I didn't say it. This is one promise I have to keep."

There was resignation in Haluk's voice. "This is folly."

"Not to me," Maggie said.

"And you're going to do this no matter what?" Haluk asked.

"Yes," Maggie said.

Haluk sighed and stood up. "Order dinner, I'll make the call."

He walked quickly through the lounge without stopping for his usual chat with the pianist, and disappeared into the lobby. Maggie nodded to the waiter, and ordered for them both.

Haluk returned just before a bevy of waiters, resplendent in white jackets and black ties, approached the table. "You have a guide. Meet him here in the morning at eight." He surveyed the trays of food. "I wasn't very hungry but I am now."

Maggie and Haluk upheld a mealtime truce. In this culture, food was to be savored and enjoyed. Early on they had declared no business conversation would be allowed. It had proven to be a good rule. The mental time out gave them each, over the years, time to process their occasional heated exchanges over how to implement some of Mr. Beyter's requests.

They watched and laughed softly at the couple in the swimming pool who were blissfully unaware that the side of the pool nearest the restaurant was a solid wall of glass. A restaurant guest dispatched a waiter to inform the amorous couple.

"How fast do you think they'll get out of the pool?" Maggie asked. She finished her last bite of kebab and sipped her sweet Turkish coffee.

"Quickly." Haluk smiled back and finished the last tidbit of his pastry. He laid out lira for the bill and offered his arm to Maggie as he walked her up the stairs to her room and opened the door.

"Are you going to be at breakfast in the morning?" She kicked off her shoes and dropped into a chair by the window.

"You've not told me anything about this guy."

Haluk narrowed his eyes. He walked to the window and leaned against the frame. "Let's see, Enver's a bit older, his mother was a nomad, he was educated in London …"

"What?" Maggie sat upright.

"Oh yes, hated it, came home, brought some English girl back from London, she left quickly, he moved back to the tribe and has cut most ties to the Western world. Exception, he does love a good suit. He is only taking you to the tribe because he respected Mr. Beyter."

"Why on earth did you pick him?" Maggie frowned. "This is important."

Haluk looked down at his shoes, out the window and finally at her. "I've known him all my life. And, since you insist on going all the way up to the ends of the earth—he's your man." He stepped over to Maggie and kissed the top of her head. "You don't have to do this. I wish you wouldn't." He moved toward the door. "Goodnight."

Maggie listened for the thunk of the door closing. She pulled the blanket off the bed, opened the window and reshuffled herself into the chair. She studied the sliver of golden moon, listened to the incoming waves slapping at the shore, and sat unmoving until the last faint star yawned its way toward morning.

The years she had spent with Mr. Beyter flitted through her mind. A scholarship based on an essay of her life had been only the beginning. She had graduated from Oklahoma State University summa cum laude with a degree in international business. She had worked first as his aide, then assistant and finally as a project manager for programs to benefit the plight of women around the world.

From the beginning Maggie had studied him with barely concealed awe. He was a courtly silver-maned lion and an understated powerhouse of knowledge. He had been a prisoner in Europe in World War II, she had heard. He had come to the university on a refugee program, learned English and had completed a bachelor's degree in less than the four years required. He had designed and developed a dependable workhorse pump used around the world. His ascent within the business world was legendary.

It was he who had instilled within her a deep respect for the proud and fierce heritage of the nomad tribes that dotted the plains and mountains of his beloved country.

Chapter Two

Maggie dozed fitfully and awoke to brush the image of Mr. Beyter back into the shadows of her mind. She couldn't afford to dwell in the past. She stifled the queasiness in her stomach, patted powder on her nose and arrived at the hotel dining room precisely at eight o'clock. Relieved to be there first, she selected her favorite outdoor spot. The curved stucco walls provided niches for small booths that offered a degree of privacy without compromising the view of courtyards. She left the space on the booth next to her for Haluk and the wrought iron chair for the stranger. Haluk would not leave her alone to deal with this man—surely.

From her vantage point, Maggie would be able to see the nomad approaching from the staircase that led to the terraced pool above, or from the dining room entrance. Masses of bougainvillea cascaded down the walls and palm trees barely moved in the moist morning air.

In a moment she watched a man ripple down the staircase. He strolled toward her with an air of success. He wore a black sport jacket over a black tee shirt, and sported tan slacks with a razor crease. His dark hair was flat and smooth, framing a face that housed eyes as black as wet onyx. He looked around and saw that Maggie was the only person on the patio. "You must be the American I am supposed to meet. I don't suppose you speak our language?" he asked, in Turkish, looking around. "Where's Haluk?"

"I do speak your language and I don't know where he is," Maggie responded in Turkish. Before she could say anything more Haluk appeared. Slightly out of breath, he slid into the booth next to her.

"Where have you been?" the Turk asked Haluk.

"Traffic and road work," Haluk said. He quickly made the introductions. "Maggie, meet Enver, the only man I trust to take you to the nomads." He turned to Enver. "This is Maggie Meadows, the American woman I told you about." He waved at a waiter and signaled for coffee.

Enver shifted the wrought iron chair with ease and sat down with cat-like grace. He turned directly toward Maggie, lit a cigarette and blew smoke upward. "So, you want to join my tribe."

"I do," Maggie said. The abruptness startled her.

"You worked in Urfa?" he asked.

"Yes," she said. "I worked the fields with the women on the farms near the Attatürk Dam. The Beyter Foundation bought milking equipment and sewing machines, and I helped establish small businesses there." She hated the defensiveness that crept into her voice. "Everyone that I worked with is still doing well."

"That's what Haluk said—you'd worked very well with the Turks there," said Enver. "We're different. We control our own destiny." He sat back and pursed his lips. Under a pale plume of smoke he eyed Maggie again. "What do you know about nomads?" he asked.

"Not as much as I'd like to know," Maggie replied evenly.

"If you come to our tribe you'll have to prove yourself to the chief before you will be taught to read the histories in our carpets." Enver leaned forward. "You'll be there to learn, to work beside our women at the looms, milk the goats, cook, preserve meat, carry water, dye the wool, and do all that our women do."

"I understand the work part. How long will it take to prove myself?" Maggie asked.

"As long as the chief wants. Our measurement of time is quite different than what you're accustomed to," Enver said.

"Will I be able to help the women with the bartering and selling if I can't start learning to read the carpets when I get there?" she asked.

"No. The chief will decide if and what you can do, and when," Enver said.

"That doesn't sound right. Mr. Beyter said I should help the women with bartering or whatever they want me to. He told me that the last time I saw him," Maggie said.

"It's not about what they want, it's about what they need that's important." Enver's voice deepened. He took a long pull on his cigarette and glanced at Haluk. "I'm very close to regretting this decision."

Haluk ran a hand through his mass of tangled hair. "Give her a chance. You told me she could go."

"If she can't agree to tribal custom, then she can't come. Six months for a foreign woman to live with us is a long time," Enver said. He stubbed out the cigarette, leaving one small ember alive. It curled its way to Maggie's nostril. "Mr. Beyter was a fine Turk who did many good things. We're proud he didn't forget us, but he stayed in America too long." Enver stood up. "Thanks for coffee."

Maggie stood up. "I can give you my answer now," she said.

"No. You *must* take the time to think about it." Enver turned to Haluk. "She won't last two months."

Haluk laughed. "You're wrong. What do I get if she stays?"

"You'll get two goats and a donkey delivered to your condo if she *doesn't* stay the full six months." Enver picked up his cigarettes. "And I'll personally deliver them."

Maggie looked from one to the other. *How could they?*

Enver turned to Maggie. "I'm going back to my village on Saturday."

"That's only three days from now," Maggie said.

"Yes, and I won't come back until September." Enver lit a cigarette and then blew smoke in Maggie's general direction. "Think about it."

Maggie watched Enver take the stairs two at a time and disappear around the corner of the hotel. "You just made a bet on me. How could you?"

Haluk waved off her indignation. "If I hadn't he would have thought I had no faith in you. Never bargain from a position of weakness." He picked up the bill. "Did he say he was leaving in three days? You can't get ready to leave that fast."

"Oh, yes I can." Maggie drummed her fingers on the table. "He thinks I'm afraid of him and that I'll back out, but that's not going to happen."

Maggie felt a stiffening of her spine that hardened her jawline. It wasn't that she couldn't go and live in the mountains. She was worried about lymphedema and a lot of other things. She missed Mr. Beyter. His death had affected her more deeply than she cared to admit.

She gathered up her key. "Let's see, I need to go to the doctor, the pharmacy and Lahli—I have to see Lahli." She mouthed a goodbye to Haluk, who was accepting change from the waiter, and headed to her suite.

Maggie made several phone calls, arranged appointments and then placed a call to reception for a bottle of wine to be delivered to her. She ran a comb through her hair and readied herself for the most important visit she would make before leaving Antalya. She slipped on sturdy clogs to walk on the narrow cobblestone streets that wound their way like carelessly strewn ribbon from the marina to the bustle of the new part of the city.

She slowed down at Omar's carpet shop as a gaggle of gray-haired women wearing black polyester slacks and white athletic shoes chattered in admiration over a pile of small rugs he had on exhibit near the doorway. Out of the line of sight of the group, Omar rolled his eyes at Maggie and feigned hopelessness in the face of American tourists. Maggie knew he made good money in the tourist trade, but he also provided good information about the quality of the carpets he sold.

She wound her way around the curved streets of Old Town, darted into a potter's stall to dodge a too-fast taxi, nodded to shop owners along the way, stopped to admire a potter's newest handcrafted pitcher, then climbed the familiar worn steps to the busy boulevard and the new part of the city.

At the top of the stairs trucks honked and cars responded. Maggie walked briskly westward threading her way among busy professional men and women to the various shops for her errands and appointments. She smiled at raven-haired schoolgirls in royal blue uniforms. A sprinkling of tourists armed with cameras and belly packs haggled with veteran street vendors selling cheap souvenirs.

It was late afternoon when Maggie rang the doorbell of Dr. Lahli Kadir, a professor of nomadic animal diseases at Akdeniz University. Lahli, twenty years her senior, had first befriended Maggie as a favor to Mr. Beyter. The friendship had deepened over the years. Lahli had become not quite a mother, not quite a mentor.

The big door opened wide. "Maggie, come in. How good it is to see you. You're back from Urfa, was it good?" Lahli asked.

"It was great. But it's nice to be back in Antalya." Maggie's eyes dwelt on the carefully coiffed white-haired woman. "You look fantastic." She hugged her hard, and was rewarded with a hug in kind.

Not to be ignored, an ancient English hunting dog nosed his way between the two of them. Maggie stooped to pat its head as it swayed precariously in the doorway near them.

"Hello, Florence, I haven't forgotten you." She offered him a treat. Lahli had rescued the male dog on a trip to Florence, Italy. She had shipped it home and given it the name of its birthplace. It was one of the things that endeared her to Maggie.

Maggie glanced around the room at the modern Danish furniture, fitting, yet spare. The blond and brown pieces showcased the intricate gold and blue weavings in the fine carpets carefully placed throughout. A familiar ache streaked its way through Maggie's being.

Why couldn't I be satisfied with a life like this?

"I have a bottle of wine stolen from the hotel cellar." She handed the bag to Lahli and leaned on the marble counter. "Kemal wasn't looking."

Lahli laughed. "Not possible. Kemal has managed that hotel for so many years I can't recall who was there before him. I know him well, and he might let you take the flowers, the bedding or even the money, but never the wine." She poured two small glasses and slid one on the counter. They lifted their glasses in a Turkish toast, "*Şerefe.*"

Together they walked to the balcony, stood arm–in–arm overlooking the green manicured lawn of Attatürk Park and the calm Mediterranean.

"It's a view I never tire of," Lahli said, "but we should talk, my dear." She led the way to one of the long comfortable sofas that faced the sea, out of the chill of the slight breeze.

They sat down on opposite ends of the sofa. Lahli patted the middle and, with a mighty effort, Florence climbed up and arranged himself with his head in her lap. Close enough to Lahli to talk in the warm circle of friendship, Maggie absently patted the old dog's haunch as he snoozed and snored.

"I heard from Haluk you're going to our Urek village." Lahli's smile began with her dark eyes.

"News travels fast. In three days, as a matter of fact," Maggie said.

"That soon? I know you wanted to stay here and recover for a few weeks. My dear, this project may very well be the hardest one you ever undertake. But—it will be the most important one you have ever done if you can complete it," Lahli said.

Maggie shook her head. "I don't know why Mr. Beyter was so insistent that I do this, and then …"

"And you promised him and now you feel you must honor his wishes?" Lahli asked.

"I don't understand it," Maggie said. "There's an entire country of women here capable of doing this in their native language."

"Mustafa Beyter singled you out because the tribe must come to trust a foreigner before they listen to one. He thinks you can do this," Lahli said. "You're a protégé of a man all the tribe knew as a childhood friend. The tribe will allow you to go to the yayla because of him, not because of you." She scratched Florence's ears. "Remember that."

Maggie swirled her wine. "I have spent so long in this country working with women like you, and men like Haluk, smart professional men who expect women to be equal—I'm

Stone the Goat

not sure I can go so far backward anymore. It's one thing for a month at a time; like on the farms near the dam, but six months ..." She looked at Lahli and sighed. "I know. I made a promise. Black and white."

Lahli folded her hands. "It is your decision to make."

"I knew you'd say that." Maggie finished her wine and begged off a second glass. "I would never have lasted here as a single woman without you."

"Widowed, my dear, and yes, you would have." Lahli tucked a strand of hair behind Maggie's ear. "How's your health?"

"I'm fine," Maggie said.

"You're sure? Got everything you need for your arm?"

"Not yet, but I've got three whole days," Maggie said dryly.

Lahli straightened Maggie's collar. "Now, do you have a guide?"

"I do. His name is Enver Ersoy and you can't believe what he did. He bet Haluk that I wouldn't stay for the whole six months, and told him if I didn't he'd bring a donkey and a goat or something and stick it in Haluk's condo. What kind of a man says a thing like that?"

Lahli leaned forward and took Maggie's hand into her own. "Enver, of course, who else would Haluk choose but Enver?" She squeezed Maggie's fingers gently. "I have known both those boys since they were children. In some ways they haven't changed. Enver will be a good guide but he is full of himself, very full."

She leaned back on the sofa, and the soft light played on

her white hair, a faraway look flitted across her slender face. "Pay his antics no mind. If I had listened to all the men who told me I could never be a professor, or bet that I wouldn't succeed, I'd still be in the mountains myself." She turned to Maggie. "Look at us. We are in a country full of smart women doing everything, but our nomad women need all the advocates they can get when it comes to preserving our culture." She squeezed Maggie's hand again. "So, go and do well. Come back and tell me your success stories."

ఌ

Maggie walked slowly back toward the comfort of the old city. She stopped in Attatürk Park and wandered through the paths. She found an empty bench near the water. Her bravado from the morning was gone. What if something happened to her? There were no medivac helicopters to airlift her from the mountain top and not a soul there she would know. If the tribe didn't want her any more than this Enver did, and if they expressed their contempt as openly, what possible good could come of this?

Maggie picked at the lint in her sweater pockets on the way to Old Town. The truth was it didn't really matter what she thought. Mustafa Beyter had asked her to do this one last thing. He had been there for her when her mother died, had given her away when she married Robert, and offered her the world of travel in her widowhood. She owed him. She kicked a pebble off the sidewalk and started down the stairs.

Chapter Three

Maggie glanced at her watch. She had been waiting for Enver for twenty minutes in the hotel's outdoor bar. A young hotel staffer plumped the thick white cushions on the wooden lounge chairs placed around the sparkling pool. She looked up at the banana yellow umbrella above her, tilted just so and the bartender busily stacking raki glasses for a later clientele. The rhythm of life in Turkey was an adjustment she had easily made. During the lags between appointments and arrival times of her Turkish counterparts, she wrote in her journal, honed her language skills reading the Turkish newspaper or found some other means to assimilate into this culture where time was not the ruler by which success was measured.

Today was different. Maggie wanted only to take care of what needed to be taken care of followed by dinner alone in her suite.

Enver arrived half an hour late and lowered himself into the bamboo chair across from Maggie. "You said you wanted to come to the Taurus Mountains," he said abruptly, "to stay with my people. You have had a chance to think about it. Do you still intend to come?" Enver asked.

Last chance. Mr. Beyter would understand.

"I intend to come," Maggie said.

Enver leaned back in the chair. "It will be hard on a woman like you, accustomed to the finer things in life." He started at her feet, shod in serviceable tan flats, took in her khaki pants and white shirt, paused at her breasts before wandering back to her face. "You can't dress like that in the village." He looked around for a waiter. "Have you ordered a drink?"

Maggie heard the resentment creep into her voice and tried to temper it. "No, I haven't. I know how to dress when I get to your village. I'm in Antalya, and this is appropriate here."

"I'm having raki." His voice was smoky and deep. "You?"

"Same."

Enver looked at her again before holding up two fingers for the bartender, "Two rakis." He leaned forward in the chair. "I've traveled the world. I know what western women expect. They lead very soft lives, like soft boiled eggs."

"You will find that isn't so," Maggie said.

"Make absolutely sure you can live without your creature comforts because I will not leave my tribe to bring you back here before September," Enver said.

"I would never ask you to. If you don't want to take me, don't; Haluk can make other arrangements for me," Maggie said.

Enver looked Maggie over once more. "It's settled then. My village is northeast of here. It will take several weeks to prepare for our trip to the upper yayla. That's high in the mountains."

"I know that," Maggie said.

Stone the Goat

He shifted in his chair. "I forget that Mr. Beyter would have told you these things."

"He did, and I'll be ready." Maggie finished her drink.

"What's a kilim?" He fired the question at her.

"A flat weave rug," she said.

"How many cotton knots in a carpet?" He fired again.

"None." Maggie's voice was strong. "Knots are wool or silk. Do you think I don't know this?"

Enver finished his raki in one swift motion and motioned to the waiter for the bill. He stood up and dropped enough lira on the table for his portion. "Three days from today." He snapped open his cigarette case on his way to the door.

Maggie fumbled in her purse, found enough lira to round out the bill, and quietly cursed all breathing men like Enver everywhere.

⁂

Maggie sat at the small desk in her suite and marked off the last of the notes and scribbles on her to-do list.

She had taken the three days before her departure to shop the streets of Antalya for the items she hoped she would need to spend six months living with the nomads. She poked at the mound of things on the bed and shook her head. How could she possibly know what she would need?

Maggie pulled two boxes and two duffel bags from the closet. The duffel bags had served her well in her trips around the globe. She wiped the dust from them, buried her face in the rich black leather, and rubbed her hands over the scars of travel. She checked the handles and zippers. Mr. Beyter had surprised her with them one year for her birthday. Throughout the years the more she traveled the fewer suitcases she carried until what she needed for her working life had been reduced to what could be placed in the battered but beautiful bags on the bed.

She stuffed the larger one with the clothes she would need: leggings, long skirts and *şalvars*—those comfortable baggy trousers with low inseams worn by rural men and women— long-sleeved shirts and vests, clogs, sweaters and slippers for the carpets. The second bag was filled with personal hygiene items: medicines, notebooks, pens, paperback classics, one set of traveling sheets, a thin faded quilt and a small feather pillow.

After a last glance around the room Maggie locked the door behind her. Dressed in sturdy canvas pants, a long tunic, good walking shoes and a jacket for the higher elevation later, she made her way to the lobby.

She turned in the heavy brass key at the marble desk. "Kemal, my bags are ready when you are."

"You're leaving us I hear." The portly hotel manager snapped his fingers, and motioned one of the bellboys toward the stairs. "Shall I hold your suite?"

She had debated that. There wasn't a suite she loved more than the one that overlooked the entrance to the hotel and the bay below. Street sweepers and shopkeepers knew to look for her in the early morning hours at the window.

"Can you keep my two boxes in the cellar again?" One day

she expected him to say no, but he hadn't yet.

"Of course, anything, but only because you teach my staff such good English," Kemal smiled at her.

"In that case, don't keep the suite. I'll be gone up to the yayla for a long time. I promise to write you a letter once a week, though." She grinned faintly at him. "I'll send them back by carrier pigeon."

They were laughing as a car stopped in front of the lobby. Maggie stepped out to see Haluk at the bottom of the steps.

"I didn't think you would be here!" Maggie said.

"I wouldn't let you leave without saying goodbye." Amidst the curious eyes of the hotel staff gathered at the door he placed his hands on her arms, pulled her to his chest and kissed her hair.

"I do plan to come back." Maggie laughed with a nervousness she hoped she didn't convey. "And you're sure there's no way to get in touch with you?"

"By phone from the village. After that it's nothing." Haluk held her close, not letting her go.

They both caught peripheral movement and turned as Enver stepped out of Omar's carpet shop with a large package in his hand. Gone were the expensive slacks and sport coat. He wore a black turban, a linen shirt and old cotton pants. He could have been any one of the farmers Maggie had met over the years.

"Good morning." He nodded to them collectively, and locked eyes with Haluk. "I see you've said your goodbyes to the American."

"Yes, I have. Promise me you'll take care of her." Haluk left a possessive arm around Maggie. "Don't let her wander off and bring her back to me safely in September."

"I will, I will," Enver said.

With a swift motion Enver picked up her bags, walked around Haluk's silver BMW and tossed them into the back of a dilapidated truck. They fell among boxes of engine oil, piles of rope, and bundles of dried flowers tucked into a corner.

"Let's go." He opened the driver side door, eased onto the seat and started the engine. Maggie wrestled with her door handle. Haluk stepped up and wrenched it open. She clambered in. He stood for a moment longer. Maggie sat on her hands to keep from stroking his safe and wonderful face.

"You can't keep taking care of me." Maggie forced a smile. "Go on, get out of here."

Haluk closed the door firmly, his eyes still on her face. "Goodbye."

Enver didn't look at her. He gunned the engine, and the truck bounced away from the hotel. He shifted gears as they merged into the traffic on the boulevard.

The morning sun poked its head through patchy clouds. In the strip of land between the mountains and the Mediterranean Sea, lumbering along the new highway, Enver broke the silence.

"So, how did you meet Mustafa Beyter?" Enver asked.

"Short or long version?" Maggie blew her nose hard.

"Short."

"At Oklahoma State University years ago. He selected me

for a scholarship. I told him I couldn't take it unless I had a job, too. He'd designed that little pump and let me help him update the marketing."

He checked his mirrors and changed lanes. "When did you learn to speak Turkish?"

"At the same time. He told me if I wanted to work in the international arena I had to learn at least three other languages."

"Did you?" He twisted his head in her direction.

She stared straight ahead. "What do you think?"

"I'm asking you."

"Turkish, Spanish, German and French," she said.

"That's four."

"I've never done exactly what I was told." The languages had come easily to Maggie. She loved the trilling of the Spanish *r*, the German back-throat sounds smartly marching into perfect sentence structure, the sensual French as chic as a black beret. But her favorite, the Turkish language, gently folded itself into a stream of vowel harmony, like water flowing over polished river stones.

The traffic flowed smoothly. Maggie noticed the new pastel yellow and pink apartment buildings. Carpets hung like limp cats over balcony rails, and women in colorful headscarves brushed them in the morning sun.

The city disappeared behind them, and Maggie's square of smudgy truck window became a panorama of orange groves and olive trees, dairy farms and highway signs. She could see the ruby glint of big tomatoes in the greenhouses along the road. She read the familiar names of the gas stations—Shell and Total—and the ones she had grown to know—*Sunpet, Yurtgaz* and *Otogaz.* She saw a billboard for Rado Watches and stared wistfully at one for *Efes* beer.

"How long have you known Haluk?" Enver's eyes didn't leave the busy highway.

Maggie thought of the Georgetown educated Haluk, a man she had seen meld easily into cultures from London to Istanbul to Santiago—a true citizen of the world.

"Seven years. Mr. Beyter introduced him to me on my first visit here. Told me he knew everyone and would make the initial introductions to the local men I needed to know."

"Have you worked with him much?"

"Quite a bit—Diyarbakir, Eskeşehir—lots of places." She smiled at the memories. "I enjoy his company."

"I noticed that when we left the hotel."

Maggie chose not to answer. Haluk was a Turk who knew how to be a gentleman. He was handsome, single and had never asked her out—not once, not ever—and although she hadn't wanted him to—she wasn't nearly ready and it would ruin a perfectly good friendship—she hated that he had never even tried. Damn.

Maggie closed her eyes to feel the lulling rhythmic rumble of the engine—and to reminisce.

☙

Haluk opened the car door on Maggie's side and helped her into the steel gray BMW.

"This is nice," she murmured as she caressed the pale leather upholstery. She stood outside his auto dealership, the largest one in Eskeşehir, a mild spring day in the making. "Why are we taking this one?"

"Well, I should drive the new cars when they come to the showroom, and we need to go to Antalya, so why not?" He adjusted the mirrors and a pair of designer sunglasses to his liking.

Hundreds of horses stamped impatiently beneath the hood as Haluk spun the car out of the parking lot. He zigged through the city traffic, singing with a song on the radio. On the outskirts of the city Maggie felt the surge of power as a straight length of road appeared.

"I think you should fasten your seatbelt." Haluk flipped off the radio as a small donkey cart came into view, "We might need to pass him."

"Did that when I got in with you," Maggie sucked in her breath as the speedometer needle curved steadily toward 180 kilometers. "Is this speed good for the new engine?" she managed to blurt out as the winds swept her words away.

"But of course." Haluk's brow furrowed as they flew by a convoy of old farm trucks, slowing down only to let an oncoming car dart back into its lane. High in the mountains the BMW loosed a throaty purr and clung to the serpentine curves like lovers reunited.

"What happens if a tire blows out right about here?" Maggie shouted above the sound of the wind.

"I will be in Paradise with seventy dark haired virgins—

what about you?"

"Just get me to the hotel." Maggie closed her eyes and prayed she wouldn't be tomorrow's headline. She held her breath until Haluk careened around the last tight corner of Old Town and coasted to a smooth stop in front of the hotel.

"Safe arrival, just as I promised." Haluk blinded her with a smile before he reached over and unlocked her door. "Out, please. I'm late for the camel race."

☙

"You're smiling in your sleep." Enver's voice brought Maggie back to the present.

"No doubt." She rubbed her eyes and squinted in the sunlight. The vision of a laughing Haluk disappeared.

Past the city of Manavgat they turned north off the busy highway and started the gradual ascent to the Urek village. Pine trees began to replace billboards, and the less traveled paved road became rougher as they climbed.

Maggie rolled down her window, the April breeze a perfect foil for the bright clear day. She felt the need to toss some words into the abyss of silence. "Can you tell me about the village?"

"You'll see it for yourself." Enver kept his eyes on the road. As it steepened, the earth lost the softness of fertile dirt and gave way to sharp stones.

Here the sky had rained rocks, and the earth had birthed an equal bounty in return. They littered the ground from pebbles to boulders, and every imaginable size in between. There weren't lush spaces of grass, just scrubby pine trees and acres of rocks as far as she could see.

Small herds of goats clicked their hooves across the rutted road, in search of the sparse grass. Herdsmen nodded to Enver as he maneuvered the truck with care.

Past another sharp curve, the edge of the road on Maggie's side disappeared from view. With a quick intake of breath, she inched her way toward the center of the truck. A wide flat area jutted out ahead. Enver pulled into it and cut the engine.

Maggie released her breath in a low whistle. A distant valley, almost hidden in the shroud of pearl gray fog lay between them and towering mountain peaks. "Is that where we're going?" Maggie pointed to the farthest peak.

"No." Enver pointed to one nearer. "It isn't far to the village, but I stop here on every trip to see my mountains." With one hand he brushed his hair back, and Maggie watched the Enver of Antalya disappear.

"How much further?" Maggie made one last attempt at polite conversation.

He hunched over the wheel and with a sudden jolt started the truck. "Soon."

Maggie leaned her head against the backrest. Each curve up the mountain took her farther away from everything she had worked for and closer to the life she had spent a lifetime leaving.

They snaked their way up the side of the mountain, glimpses of valleys and peaks with every turn. Soon, a bend in the road revealed a huddle of mottled stone houses. The first one on their right was newer, constructed of concrete blocks. It sparkled in fresh white paint. Maggie noticed the flat rooftop that held a water tank and a clothesline where a trio of small scarves moved half-heartedly in the breeze. Trees provided shade to the front porch and a chicken coop sat under an olive tree nearby.

"We're here," Enver announced, as he brought them to an abrupt halt next to a truck as decrepit as his. "You'll stay with Ali and Ashil. They're my cousins." He rested his arms on the steering wheel and looked straight ahead. "I'm responsible for you. Don't embarrass me or make me sorry I brought you here."

A flush of anger swept up Maggie's tightened chest. She turned to look at him fully. "I won't embarrass you. Just remember, Enver, we're equal."

"Not in my world."

Before Maggie could respond, a woman not much taller than she bounced from the house. Her cheeks were stained with a healthy redness and her brown button nose was bright with sweat.

Maggie took it all in. The headscarf she wore was tucked behind her ears, revealing her full and smiling face. The longsleeved blouse, a rose and floral print was stuffed inside a brown cotton şalvar. The şalvar had brown sunflowers cascading down its length. Maggie adored the voluminous creation of pant and skirt which provided guaranteed modesty regardless of the position nomadic women sometimes found themselves.

Stone the Goat

The woman smiled shyly at Maggie. "Welcome to our village and my home," she said.

Maggie listened carefully. Each region of the country spoke with a different accent, and it was always difficult at first to understand the language. This would require all the skill she possessed.

"It's good to see you, Ashil. This is the American woman Mr. Beyter gave to Haluk to watch. Her name is Maggie." Enver scooped up Maggie's bags and set them on the porch.

"Please come in," Ashil said. She moved gracefully to the concrete porch, covered in rugs and pillows.

An old man in a brown fez stepped outside and greeted Enver in a gravelly voice. They embraced and then fell into a quiet conversation as they walked past Enver's truck.

Enver spoke over his shoulder at Ashil. "After you've milked tomorrow I'll take her to meet the chief."

Maggie stood silently as her only link to the outside world moved slowly up the dusty road without a backward glance.

You've been alone before. You'll be fine.

The sour taste of fear begged to differ.

Ashil slid out of her shoes and left them on the edge of the porch. "We have a lot to do because our trip to the yayla is coming soon." She bent to arrange the pillows. "I've made a supper for you and me. Ali is with the chief today." She stood up and pointed to the pile of pillows. "Please sit here."

As a guest, Maggie followed cultural protocol and didn't offer to help. She thought of her first visits to Lahli's house in Antalya and how formal they were. In time, she had been invited to cook with Lahli in her kitchen. She had even dog-sat for Florence when Lahli needed to be away. None of it had happened quickly.

Maggie rested on the rugs. They were called kilims in Turkey. The simple flat weave reminded her of the braided rag rugs her mother had made. Maggie kept them in storage in the States. She leaned on large comfortable pillows and admired the almond tree that shaded the porch. It had a sturdy trunk and bright green leaves; the branches laden with unripened nuts. She touched the rough fabric of an indigo pillow, the deepest blue she had ever seen. Tightly woven, each row was perfect, ending in an ebony fringe. She stared at the kilim beneath her and soaked up the boldness and geometric pattern design. It was white, black, gold, red, blue, brown, green and purple. Maggie inspected it more closely. If nomad women wove their lives into the carpets and kilims, what was this one saying?

The long day settled into Maggie's limbs. She leaned back into the pillows and closed her eyes. She heard a rooster crow near the end of the porch. She opened her right eye to see him puff out his black feathers, crow again and chase a small brown hen into the chicken coop that squatted under a bushy olive tree near the stone fence. With a flurry of wings the hen clucked him away indignantly.

Maggie jumped up as Ashil backed out of the door with a large metal tray. "Please, at least let me do this." She lifted the pink and white checked tablecloth off the top of the food and spread it over the rainbow of rugs on the porch.

Ashil reached up and plucked almonds from the tree that touched the porch and filled her apron. She tilted the corner of the apron and dropped them, like a waterfall of green marbles, into a bowl. She handed one to Maggie. "Please, try it with a little salt. We like them green and when they ripen too."

Maggie bit into the crisp tartness of the almond. "It's good." She reached for two more, salted them, and crunched in enjoyment. "They're very good." The smile on Ashil's face broadened.

Ashil served lunch from the large metal tray. She selected a boiled egg ready to shell, small pieces of ripe tomato, thinly sliced cucumbers, yogurt, and a slice of honey comb dripping with golden honey and arranged it on a plate. A large platter of flat bread with a green filling sat near her. "This is spinach and goat cheese," she said, and placed two on each plate. She passed one to Maggie and kept one for herself.

Ashil handed Maggie a small clear glass. She poured dark amber tea into it, leaving room to add hot water and sugar. Next, she offered boiling water, and Maggie watched as she slowly poured a stream into the glass. When the color turned the amber that Maggie loved, she nodded and Ashil stopped. She then added water to her own. Maggie picked up two sugar cubes from a small bowl and dropped them into the steaming glass of tea. She closed her eyes and sipped.

The tea ritual was the same, from the cities of the west to the villages in the east. For a country noted for its incomparable coffee, it was tea that lubricated the fabric of life.

Maggie could tell Ashil was bursting to ask her questions. She had lived among the Turks long enough to know that age, children, occupation were all questions that could be asked in introductory meetings. But she was happy to rest. She had bounced for hours in the truck, and the comfortable pillows and kilims were a welcome relief. The time to herself in the truck, and Enver hadn't said much, had helped her mentally prepare for the awkwardness of meeting strangers, which she had learned over time, to do.

"Your rugs are beautiful." Maggie feasted her eyes on the colors and designs. "I look forward to reading them."

Ashil blushed. "Thank you. Can you read them at all?"

"Some. I know the general motifs but not the specifics of the old carpets."

"I'll help teach you the old ways when we get to the yayla." Ashil wiped her hands on her apron. "I like that you're going to live with Ali and me." She blushed again. "I have a lot of questions, but I have a lot of work, too."

The late afternoon sun dipped behind a mountain peak, and the air grew cooler. Ashil quickly finished her tea and picked up the tray. She wouldn't let Maggie help her through the door. "I'll just put the things away." Maggie leaned back into the pillows and her eyelids fluttered.

Ashil returned just as Maggie stifled a deep yawn. Ashil stood a moment, as if deciding what to do with her. She wrapped a bundle of dark blue wool around her left arm and picked up her wooden hand spindle. "I'll take you to your room." Maggie followed her to the rear of the house and a small room near the staircase. "You can rest here, and tomorrow I'll take you to meet the other women, and see the village." She smiled once more. "And now I'm going to weave." Twirling her spindle, she walked quickly up the dusty road and disappeared around a curve.

Left alone, Maggie inspected the small clean room. A bowl of green almonds and a glass jar of salt rested on a small bureau in one corner. A table with an oil lamp sat within reach of three plush carpets stacked in an opposite corner. Through one large window she saw a dusty road and an old stone house far beyond.

Tired but curious, Maggie retraced her steps to the porch. She walked toward the chicken coop and found a small gray donkey grazing just beyond. A thick goat skin covered his back, wool side down, and a wooden saddle sat firmly in place. She stepped closer to inspect it. The donkey ignored her and nosed among the stones for the green tendrils of grass. The craftsmanship of the saddle was crude but effective; wooden slats curved and slotted together to provide a seat for the rider without hurting the animal. Other forays into the heartland of the country had offered her ample opportunity to ride such a donkey. It certainly was better than walking.

A small boy trotted up the road and over to the donkey. He paused, looked Maggie up and down, and then wordlessly reached for the donkey's bridle.

"Hello," Maggie spoke in clear Turkish.

The boy ignored her just as the donkey had. She watched them disappear around the bend.

Head down, Maggie shuffled back to her room. She opened the smaller duffel bag and unfolded the faded quilt and set of travel sheets. She stepped into the hall. Ashil had pointed out the two living rooms earlier. The first one had two sofas, two chairs and a wood burning stove. The second one held a small sofa and a large loom. There wasn't any need to point out to whom that room belonged.

Directly across the hall from Maggie's room was the lavatory. There, a pitcher of water, an enamel wash basin and a thick cotton towel had been laid out for her. She squatted over the white ceramic hole in the floor. A slight twinge reminded her that forty wasn't twenty. She wasn't old by any means—just old enough to have a past and young enough to have a future—that's what Lahli always said.

Back in the room she slipped into her pajamas, climbed between the sheets, and stared at the wall. She pulled the quilt to her cheek and lay her head on a soft flannel square. It was faded, a long ago yellow, with a faint pink rose and a fainter green stem. If she closed her eyes she could see her mother, head bent over the small square of Maggie's worn-out pajamas, giving each piece a new life in a quilt. Tiny stitches bound the scraps together, and in that stitching, bound Maggie and her mother to each other even now.

Five months and twenty-nine days.

The long fall into backwardness had begun.

Chapter Four

MAGGIE LIFTED HER head and sniffed. Someone was cooking. She heard sheep shuffle past her window, and peeked through a thin curtain to see a clear morning. A young herder nudged a stubborn brown ewe back into the fold. He stooped to pat her on the head, and the flock of sheep, mixed with a few mottled goats, flowed around them in a slow wave.

Maggie rubbed the sleep out of her eyes. A cup of coffee would be heaven. She spent ten minutes in deep neck and shoulder exercises. She put on the şalva*r* pants and slipped into her bra, instinctively scanning the room for a mirror. She buttoned a loose blouse. Without a mirror she would never know if her breasts were even or not.

౿

"Hi Maggie," the mammogram nurse smiled as she reached for the chart. "Has it been a year already?"

"Yes." Maggie focused on the ugly machine before her. "I really don't like coming here, know that?"

"It's the pits."

"I'm always nervous." Maggie picked at a cuticle.

The nurse positioned the machine. "Two lumpectomies

will do that." It whirred and clicked until she completed a series of images. Long moments passed. "I'm taking these to radiology now," she said, careful not to look up.

Maggie sat down hard in the overstuffed pink chair, pulled her knees up to her chin and the thin robe taut around her. She shivered, concentrated on the deep red of her toenails and said aloud to the wall, "Well, this can't be good."

The nurse returned. "There isn't any reason you can't see what Dr. Steward has found. Come on." She adjusted Maggie's robe and they disappeared into the disinfectant scented grid of corridors of the hospital.

"Morning, Maggie." The white-haired doctor patted a chair next to his. He waited until she was situated, then leaned forward and adjusted the film. "You've been down this road before, so let's just skip the damned wait-a-week-to-hear crap." With a pen, Dr. Steward slowly pointed out the tumor in Maggie's left breast. "Almost identical to your mother's." He waited a moment to see that she understood, then laid his arm around her shoulder and squeezed gently. "You can cry, kick and scream if you want to. I'll hold you."

Maggie vaguely heard something about him calling her husband, Robert.

"Doctor Denton will call you tomorrow after he's reviewed this and tell you what you'll have to do." Dr. Steward took her arm and they walked slowly down the hall. The mammo nurse joined them. Dr. Steward waved his ham-sized paws and shooed the nurse away. "I'm walking her back," he said. He shoved his glasses back up his nose. "Jesus Christ, some days I hate this job."

Robert arrived. He drove Maggie home and carried her from the car to their big white bed. In his khaki workpants and steel-toed boots he cradled her there until her ragged sobs waned into slow rhythmic breathing.

☙

With a sigh, Maggie gave the bra a hard tug and finished dressing. She followed her nose to the back of the house. In the kitchen, a rough wooden table was pushed up against the far wall. A gray stone mortar and pestle sat on one corner, a bucket of water, nearly full, and a bowl of tomatoes filled up the remaining space. A wooden cupboard with mesh screen door panels was full of copper pots and pans. Tin plates and trays were stacked closely together. The bottom shelf had cloth bags filled with what Maggie thought was flour by the tiny white spill on the floor.

The smell of food was not coming from the kitchen. Maggie looked out the back door. A few feet away a large stone hut abutted a rough rock wall that stood as a sentinel at the back of the house. A curl of smoke meandered from an opening in the top.

Maggie stepped from the kitchen to the hut and stuck her head inside. "Hello."

Ashil smiled a greeting in return. She sat on her knees dusting off the bread-making dough board. With nimble fingers she picked up the last piece of flat bread from a hot dome-shaped metal plate, stacked it on a tray with several more, slid the board under the low table and laid the rolling pin on top.

"Enver says you're going to meet the chief today after we finish the milking." She stood and shook her apron. A dust storm of flour breathed new life into the dying embers of the small fire. "He says you have to learn to milk here before we go to the yayla, and that you'll probably make lots of mistakes."

"I'm sure he's right," Maggie said.

"You'll have to cover your hair." Ashil turned toward the door. "I'll get a scarf."

"I'll—never mind," Maggie smiled. Better to use the one offered by Ashil.

Maggie blew out a long breath. The other Turkey, the modern one she had left to come here, was far removed from this custom. Most of the business women she dealt with—Lahli included—never wore a scarf. They were as well dressed and as stylish as any of the women in Vienna or Milan. At least the nomads didn't cover their faces. She should be thankful for that.

Ashil returned with a mouse brown cotton scarf. Maggie dutifully wrapped it around her head and tied it into a knot at the nape of her neck. The absence of mirrors for six months might turn out to be a good thing.

They walked quickly up the dirt road to a group of women huddled together near a stone house at the side of the road. Maggie slowly processed the assortment of blue, black, green şalvars; red, brown, yellow blouses; pink, black, gray sweaters; green dotted, blue flowered and black checked vests and multi-floral printed aprons. They wore blue plastic flat shoes or brown sandals with socks. Ashil's wildly mixed colors and patterns were no longer a bit out of place. Maggie glanced down at her brown şalvar, tan blouse and darker brown vest. She was the color of dirt.

"This is the American woman that Enver brought," Ashil said. "Her name is Maggie Hanim. I told you about her." Ashil seemed pleased with her status as Maggie's keeper. "She'll stay with us until the olives get ripe in the autumn. She's going to the yayla with us and will live with Ali and me."

The women eyed Maggie like cautious deer at the edge of a lake.

The frowns that crossed their faces told her it might just be a good idea to accept the 'Hanim,' a traditional title of respect for women. "You don't have to call me Miss," Maggie said and smiled at them. "I'm pleased to meet you. I worked many years with Mr. Mustafa Beyter. He told me stories about his mother and that she was a member of this tribe." Maggie saw the old woman nod. "He asked me to come here to live and work with you, to learn to read your carpets." Maggie stopped talking. These were not a people of haste—that she had learned from Mr. Beyter—and friendships would not easily be forged. There was so much more she wanted to say, but a certain amount of personal reserve was expected. Patience. It had grown out of necessity.

Ashil began the introductions. "This is the elder in our tribe, Hala."

Maggie extended her hand and looked deep into the black

eyes of the leathery old woman. A map of the world was etched in the fine lines on her face. Sprouts of gray hair stood proudly on her chin, and her thin lips hovered toward a smile. She did not offer her hand, but nodded her acknowledgement.

The other women greeted her at once in a cacophony of hellos, I welcome you, it's my turn, how do you do, nice to meet you, don't step on my şalvar, how are you—all of them jostling for a position to catch Maggie's eye.

Ashil quickly introduced the three women nearest her. "This is Tamay, our cheese maker, Zeynep our bread maker and Sema, who is the fastest weaver."

Tamay, a round woman with perfect teeth and a beautiful smile and Zeynep, a slender woman with sweeping eyelashes smiled and nodded. The sturdy one called Sema simply stood and looked at Maggie.

Ashil picked up her buckets. "Let's milk. Enver's coming soon." She motioned to Maggie and walked swiftly up the road. "We can talk at Hala's later today when we weave."

The clump of women followed more slowly and moved as one toward the goats that were stirring restlessly in the corral.

The location of the corral was a sizeable area backed into a stony rise that provided natural fencing for the rear of the enclosure. A low fence of dry rocks formed the front of the pen. A long shed squatted in the middle of the corral, topped with woven pine tree branches to provide shade for the goats and their kids.

Inside the gate Maggie stepped carefully, unsure of her

Stone the Goat

footing on the unforgiving stones. Ashil had moved quickly into the shed and was of sight. Maggie lagged behind.

A snort caused Maggie to turn. The biggest ram she had ever seen stopped within arm's reach. He stood waist high to her and eyed her warily. No further, stranger, he seemed to say. Frozen in place, her eyes swept over his long straight hair. It was white, except for tufts of golden hair that fell over each hoof and hindquarters. He snorted again and tossed his large curved horns in a show of menacing superiority. Maggie sucked in her breath and held it, not daring to move until Ashil returned.

Ashil re-appeared from the shed with two tin buckets in one hand. "Go." She slapped the ram on the butt with the other hand as she walked past him. He trotted off with an imperial air. Maggie expelled a long breath of relief.

Ashil waded into a sea of goats; brown, cream, white, and every combination in-between.

Maggie moved closer. "How do I help you?"

Ashil pointed to a brown ewe. "That one. Stick this pan of food under her nose and bring her here," she said. She had found a clean flat space on the hard ground, gathered up her şalvar, and sat down. "I'm ready."

Maggie shoved the battered tin pan under the ewe's nose and walked quickly toward Ashil.

Cross-legged, Ashil pulled the goat's rump to her; put a bucket between its legs; leaned into its rump—to keep it from kicking; slid her arms under its belly; and began pulling the udders in a steady motion. Smooth streams of frothy milk splashed into the bucket while the goat munched on the grain. Maggie made mental notes of what she saw. The key to success was always in the details.

Ashil motioned Maggie to bring her another. All around them other women were partaking in the same ritual.

"We won't take all the milk," Ashil explained. "We'll leave some for the babies." She moved a full bucket to the side and reached for another one.

Maggie lost count of the goats she drew to Ashil's ready hands. After the last one Ashil stood up and dusted off her clothes with a handkerchief from her pocket. She walked back to the pen and sprang the latch to release a deluge of hungry kids from the shed. They spilled over the rocks and in a crescendo of frenzied bleating found their mothers. The ewes stooped low to nibble grass as their offspring suckled hungrily on teats of warm milk.

The milking done, the goats scattered to eat and the women divided up the collected milk between them. Each woman carried two buckets in each hand as they wound their way down the hill toward the houses, peeling off until there was only Ashil and Maggie on the hard road. Maggie's hands hurt from the narrow handles pressed into her fingers. She set the buckets down and stopped to massage them.

Ashil turned her hands over to show Maggie the row of calluses across her palms. "Soon it won't hurt so much," she said.

At the house Ashil moved quickly. "We'll talk later." She poured a bucket of milk into a stone jar. "The men don't like to be kept waiting."

"Where are they?"

"Up in the village," Ashil said. She placed a cloth on the jar and looked up. "Enver's coming for you."

Maggie turned as the lithe figure moved toward her. His dusty brown britches stopped just below his knees, and kissed the long socks that rose to meet them. Tribal socks, she was sure, deep blue, burgundy and cream with some motif at the top she couldn't read. He wore a rough wool tunic and a black turban on his hair.

Enver stopped at the edge of the road. "Come," he said. He turned and headed back to the village.

And what if I don't want to?

"Go," Ashil said, giving Maggie a gentle push and a reassuring smile.

Maggie hurried to keep up with Enver's long stride. They walked back past the corral that housed the goats, and past several bee hives sitting among a stand of olive trees. The hives were white wooden boxes, similar to the ones she had seen in many rural areas. A bee keeper, his face and neck covered in a protective hat, slowly pulled up a screen covered in golden honey and gently moved the bees with his hands. That explained the fresh honey she and Ashil had had in their meal.

The houses in the village were stone and adobe, bleached golden by the sun.

Maggie pointed to the houses. "Who lives in these?"

"The people too old to go to the yayla or the ones who stay and tend our summer crops," Enver pointed to a dark stone building, "That's our school," he said.

Enver kept a step ahead of Maggie. They walked further into the center of the village. A well gurgled water into a concrete water trough. Young children bustled about with copper pots and clay jars and their infectious laughter caused Maggie to smile.

In the square, a small mosque and a building that might be the general store formed a half circle around a black goat-hair tent. It teemed with men gathered outside, smoking cigarettes and sipping glasses of tea. "Wait here," Enver said and disappeared into the tent, followed by the men who never raised their eyes to look at her.

She could hear the murmur of voices. She strained to hear Enver's, but couldn't distinguish it from the others. The children at the well peeked at her from behind their hands. They pointed and giggled among themselves before scampering off in six directions sloshing water up and down their legs.

Maggie rubbed her arms. It was chilly at this hour of the morning. The little store, if that's what it was, had burlap bags of goods stacked outside and a cigarette sign in the window. She counted a dozen houses close to the small school and the mosque. The winding streets were only wide enough for a man and his donkey, or two people to pass each other.

Unlike Ashil's house, which was newer and only one story, these houses were two levels. The villagers lived on the upper floor accessed by steep staircases of stone or concrete along an outer wall. Maggie could see a donkey and four chickens underneath one house. Another had burlap bags, tipped sideways and piled in the corner. They were stuffed with wool.

Stone the Goat

Three tiny girls, not yet school age, peered at her through the wooden railings of one house. Maggie stood without moving and smiled at the girls. They scurried like frightened mice up the stairs and past an open door.

Maggie stood on one foot and then the other, counting the tiles on the mosque roof. Eventually Enver stepped out of the tent and held the flap open for an older man. Muscular and swarthy, he moved with a commanding grace to the center of the square. He cupped his hand to light a cigarette and stared at Maggie over the glow.

Maggie shivered at the fierce eyes, hard lines and deep crevasses of his face. This must be the chief. She fought a desire to run as fast as she could down the mountain side and back to the safety of Haluk and Antalya. She forced herself to stand still. The man's hair was the color of ashes, his white beard streaked with faint yellow. Dark tobacco-looking stains spotted the tips of his moustache. He smelled like the wet corner of an old barn.

"I am Abdul, chief of the Urek tribe. I've heard of the death of Mustafa Beyter. He was my father's friend, and a friend of mine. That's why you can be here," he said. He picked tobacco from his teeth and flicked it away. "Where are your brothers? They should be watching you."

"I don't have any brothers," Maggie said.

"Is that why Mustafa Beyter had you, gave you away to Haluk and Haluk gave you to Enver?" Abdul's eyes flitted over Maggie.

A slow burn started somewhere in Maggie's gut and enveloped her. "Mr. Beyter didn't giv—".

"I do this for Mustafa Beyter," the chief said, "and only for him. When you work as hard as our women I might let you read our carpets." The chief stared at her vest. "If you can't do it, say so now, before we go to the yayla."

Maggie smothered the instant loathing in her voice. She addressed the chief in the old polite form of greeting, "Abdul Bey, I am—"

"Go. I've said what I have to say." He dismissed her with an impatient wave of his hand. Maggie looked for Enver. He had joined the men who had gathered near the tent entrance to listen and he didn't look her way.

Maggie turned on her heel and steamed her way back toward Ashil's house. A truck, similar to the one Enver had driven from Antalya, was parked on the side of the road just out of the village. She glanced both ways, saw no one coming and gave the closest tire one swift kick.

At Ashil's house she sprinted up the stairs. Ashil was on the roof, hanging clothes on lines that stretched from the legs of the water barrel to the olive tree. Maggie grabbed a handful of clothes pins.

Ashil squinted in the morning sun and stopped scrubbing clothes on a rippled wash board. "How was your time with the chief?" Ashil asked.

"Wonderful." Maggie picked up a rinsed shirt with one hand and shook it out with a crisp snap. She hung it up by its tail and shoved a clothespin on either end. "According to the chief, Mr. Beyter gave me to Haluk and Haluk gave me to

Enver. Imagine that. I'm owned by Enver." She snapped open another shirt.

Ashil smiled and nodded. "That's good. Enver understands strange women. He brought a woman back here from when he went away. She didn't like us and didn't stay."

Maggie vaguely remembered something Haluk had said … what was it … something about Enver coming back from England with a woman … "So that's it," Maggie muttered, "some other woman can't take it and I pay for it."

Maggie plunged her hands deep into her pockets. She was still smarting from the snubbing of the chief. It wasn't Ashil's fault the chief was a certifiable ass and Enver and up and coming one. She took a deep breath. "May I help you wash?"

"Of course," Ashil moved from the wash tub to the rinsing one. "Do you wash like this in America?"

"Not anymore, but I do know how." Maggie lifted a blouse from the soaking tub. She pulled on her childhood experiences, turned it inside out, placed the dirty collar on the ripples of the washboard and rubbed fiercely. Memories of old sharecropper houses insulated with cardboard, heated by wooden stoves and illuminated with sooty coal oil lamps muscled their way to the surface of her mind. She clubbed them back and scrubbed harder, and harder still. Finished, she tossed it into the clear water for rinsing. She stuck her arm back into the tub for the next article of clothing.

Enver hadn't said a word to the chief. Not a peep, nothing in her defense, nothing about the real relationship between her and Mr. Beyter, or Haluk.

"This is very good." Ashil dipped the blouse up and down, swirled it around in the clear water, then hand wrung it out. She hung it with the others on the clothesline. "But there's no hurry."

Maggie let the suggestion go unanswered. Thankfully Ashil didn't need to fill the space with conversation. Maggie scrubbed in a controlled frenzy until there were no more dirty clothes to be seen.

You shouldn't have done that.

She touched the slight swelling and felt the tightness in her left underarm. Doesn't matter, this is your life until September and this is one promise you are going to keep.

Chapter Five

A FITFUL NIGHT and a throbbing arm encased in a compression sleeve did little to cause Maggie to awake in a better frame of mind. She rubbed the stretched-out spandex of the flesh colored sleeve that extended from her wrist to her shoulder. She had been smart to buy two of them before she left Antalya. With the lymph nodes in her left arm removed following a radical mastectomy, Maggie's ability to purify her body of bacteria and viruses through her lymphatic system had been compromised. It was the reason Lahli had pressed her about her health before she left Antalya. Haluk had reminded her, too.

And what had she done? She had scrubbed clothes far beyond her arm's capacity for such repetitive motion—lymphedema, the swelling that followed, was a serious concern. Maggie had allowed the chief to rile her beyond reason. She had done this—Maggie inspected her arm—to herself. Never again.

Today she would start the nomad-woman processing of Maggie Meadows. She would keep her temper under control, do what she was told, and return to Antalya at the end of this sojourn having achieved success. She would blot the chief and

Enver out of her mind. Yes, it would be mind over matter.

She dressed carefully, and pulled her long-sleeved blouse down to her finger tips. The compression sleeve was not something she wanted to share or explain to anyone.

At the outdoor kitchen hut she could see, just inside, old carpets with only memories of color covered the hard ground. A small fire sputtered, and the smoke meandered its way up and out of an opening in the far corner of the hut. A cast iron Dutch oven sat off to the side, and the smell of something wonderful hovered around the heavy cover. Next to it were three red apples and a baby blue sweater.

"Hello." Maggie stepped inside to see Ashil sitting on her knees in front of a low wooden table.

Ashil smiled at Maggie. "Good morning. Did you sleep well?"

"Well enough," Maggie said.

Ashil tucked her headscarf back behind her ears. "The chief says I have to teach you how to make bread today," she paused, "it's a lot to learn all at once."

"Yes, it is, but I can do it." The small fire offered warmth and the smell of freshly cooked bread filled the hut. The kindness in Ashil's voice allayed some of the flitting fears Maggie had about her place in the life of this nomad camp for six months.

"Sit here." Ashil gently patted the carpet beside her. Humming, she reached over and added more twigs to the small fire and blew hard. She took a handful of flour and sprinkled it over the table; it's top worn to a smooth finish, and pinched off a lump of dough from a pan nearby. With a narrow rolling rod, she flattened and coaxed the dough into a thin piece the size of a large pizza. "This is yufka. It's made from flour, salt and water."

Ashil picked up the dough with the rod and spread it flat on a round metal convex sheet to cook. "Yukfa lasts a long time. We'll eat this on the way to the yayla." She flipped the bread over and laid it down gently to cook on the opposite side. "The shepherds and sheep herders take it with them when they go with the sheep." She slipped the rod under one end of the piece and used her finger to lift it off the metal cooking sheet and add it to a stack she had prepared earlier. "Now, you do it." She relinquished the rod.

Maggie took the rod and lightly floured the board. She stuck her hand into the soft mound of dough, and pinched off a handful. A few rolls with the rod and she stopped to inspect her work. It was a pathetic pancake, not a sleek piece ready for the cooking sheet. Encouraged by Ashil's smile, she tried again. "I can do this."

Ashil leaned forward and placed her hand over Maggie's. Slowly she applied the proper pressure, and Maggie's hand began to make a smooth, thin oval. "I learned this from my mother's mother." She continued to guide Maggie's hands. "Do it again." They rolled the rod, hand over hand, until Maggie caught the rhythm. Ashil moved away and stoked the fire.

Maggie misjudged the size of the dough ball at first, but soon developed an eye for the correct size to fit exactly on the table top.

Ashil sat nearby and pushed a plunger into a *kovan*, a hollowed-out stump used to churn butter. "In the autumn, when the leaves are brown, you'll be good at that," Ashil said. She picked up a large piece of the still-warm bread and handed it to Maggie. "For you."

Maggie chewed the big bite of bread, and Ashil laughed as Maggie licked a crumb from the corner of her lip.

☙

The roof of Ashil's house quickly became Maggie's favorite place to gain perspective. From there, she could see down the road and mountain side, the olive and almond trees scattered about near houses, and bee hives tucked in between them. Up the road, she could see two trucks similar to the one Enver had driven from Antalya, sitting on the side of the road in front of a large stone house. The back side of Ashil's house was positioned near a steep rise that had a stone fence meandering up as far as she could see. Maggie could look down onto the roof of the cooking hut, and see into the bed of Ali's blue truck. Her world seemed bigger from the rooftop.

Today, her job was to lay out kilims and arrange the yufka to dry. This bread was for the trip to the yayla. Maggie hefted a basket filled with the aromatic bread, climbed the stairs and set the basket down. Ashil was humming in the hut below.

Maggie spread the colorful rugs in the warm sun. She placed all the rounds of bread out in neat rows on top of them and stepped back to review her work.

Stone the Goat

Perhaps this wasn't going to be so bad. She had expected the chief to not want her. Mr. Beyter had always said a chief had the hardest heart, the last to change. Enver had disappeared into the mystery of tribal manhood; she saw him in passing, or at the well, but he didn't stop to speak to her. It still irked her that he could have explained her situation to the chief, and hadn't. But Ashil and the other women she had met seemed open to a budding friendship.

Ashil called to her from the hut. "Are you finished?" She leaned out and hung her apron on a wooden hook on the outside wall. "Enver said to show you the carpets we're weaving in the village. Can you be ready soon?"

"I'm finished up here." Maggie slipped the empty basket over her arm.

A few minutes later, she walked with Ashil toward the village. She touched her head to see that her headscarf was secure. She hated it; her head was already getting hot under the heavy thing. Maybe she could negotiate the scarf wearing and just wear her old Tilley hat instead.

They walked along the road and saw the houses Maggie had missed the previous day in her struggle to keep up with Enver on the way to meet the chief. They arrived at a brown stone one with a blue door. "This is Sema's house." Concrete stairs led up to the living quarters, and Maggie could see large bags of wool stored in the area beneath. A dog scratched himself, and a donkey brayed, tethered to a nearby tree.

Maggie recognized Sema, the village's best weaver according to Ashil, sitting in front of a large vertical loom. Balls of wool hung from the wooden crossbar at the top.

Sema saw them and stood up. "Please come up, join me for tea."

They climbed the stairs, and Ashil sat down on the pillow vacated by Sema. "Enver told me to bring Maggie Hanim to see what the women are weaving." She looked at the large flat weave rug hanging on the loom.

Sema ran her hand roughly over the portion she had completed. "It's a kilim for the big markets in Antalya. Look at this bad wool." She pointed to the mauve spools at the top of the loom. "We would only stuff pillows with it." She shook her head in disgust. "Who would want this weak color? Not a tribe I know." She left to get the tea.

Maggie had seen many carpets and kilims at Omar's carpet shop and in towns and villages from the Black Sea to the Mediterranean, from Istanbul to the eastern border of the country. Omar and Mr. Beyter had taught her how to look for quality. This kilim was made of wool taken from the second shearing of sheep. The weaving wasn't tight. It was evident that this piece was not an important one.

Sema returned with the tea and sat down near Ashil. She picked up her spindle and twirled as she talked. "These kilims make me good money. It gives me what I need for Leslihan's dowry."

Ashil sipped her tea. "Leslihan is Sema's daughter. She's getting married this summer in the yayla. We're all making pieces for her hope chest."

Maggie listened as the women spoke animatedly of the

Stone the Goat

bridal trousseau, pillow covers, water bags, and camel blankets all to be made for the bride.

When the tea had been consumed, Ashil said their goodbyes and she and Maggie repeated the same ritual in the homes of Zeynep and Tamay, each woman offering a different reason for the poor quality of wool stretched tightly on their vertical looms.

"Does everyone weave for the markets?" Maggie noticed at other looms sitting beneath trees, where young girls worked quickly tying knots in large carpets, and old women sat spinning wool.

"A lot of them do. It isn't hard work and they need money." Ashil stopped on the road. "Those carpets under the trees are for the families to pass down. Those are our history carpets." She twisted the tip of her scarf. "I don't have a son or a daughter to weave for, so I just weave for myself, and if I have too many carpets I trade them or sell them to buy pots and spoons." A tight smile crossed her lips. "But mine don't sell so well. People don't like the colors that we use in our tribe."

"No, they want colors that match the colors in their homes." Maggie almost said décor, but caught herself in time. Word choice fatigue was setting in.

"I don't have a daughter either," Maggie felt compelled to add. She had promised Robert they would start a family soon, it just hadn't been soon enough. "And I don't have a son."

☙

Maggie tiptoed carefully up the staircase. She wrapped a

woolen shawl around her shoulders, sat on a water bucket and listened to the rooster give the dawn its wake-up call. The sun soon followed. A band of light flowed from the mountain tops, down the valley and over the roof, warming Maggie in her solitary perch. The rooster eyed her from the slats of his side of the chicken coop, and she could hear the hens clucking. Eggs were imminent.

In the week she had been in the village, she had met all the women, said little and worked hard. Mr. Beyter had told her those two things would endear her to the farmers and nomads. The sage advice had worked in Urfa and other points east, and seemed to be working here.

She heard stirring in the house below. The roof was peaceful, the one place she could be alone. With a sigh she headed down the stairs.

After a breakfast of cheese, honey, olives, bread and tea, Ali left to work with the many flocks of sheep and goats.

Ashil and Maggie joined the women at the corral to milk, and then returned home to churn butter. They talked easily as Maggie pumped the plunger up and down in the kovan.

"Let's see what we have." Ashil lifted the wooden perforated paddle and scooped out the butter. She pressed it with a wooden spoon and patted it into a round form. She dipped a cup into the churn and brought it up full of milk. "We call this *ayran*. It makes you full and happy."

"We call it buttermilk." Maggie tasted the drink from the cup Ashil offered. It was thick and tasty. "It's good. Mr. Beyter called this the drink of the gods."

Stone the Goat

The sun grew warmer. Ashil sought out the shade of the porch. "We'll sit a while." She picked up her knitting and hummed under her breath.

It was a relief to sit. Maggie enjoyed thinking in English and thinking about nothing. A week into her stay, Maggie ached in muscles that had been too long on hiatus. Every day had brought something new to learn.

"Hala told me one of my jobs is to teach you how to knit socks," Ashil laughed. "Everyone wants you to know everything, and they want me to be the teacher."

"I may not be very good at it." Maggie pulled an almond off the tree and handed it to Ashil, snapped one off for her and sat down beside her. Ashil assembled the five needles used for socks. She pulled out some dull white wool and quickly started one for Maggie.

"Old wool for beginners," Ashil handed it over with a smile. She sat back against the thick pillows and picked up a long sock from her basket. Her hands flew through the stitches.

"Could I do something else? Embroider, maybe?" Maggie asked.

There was no room for negotiation in Ashil's kind voice. "No. You must do this to be nomad woman."

Maggie fumbled with her needles. "What's that pattern in the sock you're knitting?"

"It's a ram's head. It means we have a good life. These are for Ali," Ashil explained. "I knit him long ones for up in the yayla. It gets so cold up there when they sleep with the sheep." She lifted the nice white sock for Maggie to see. "Warm feet make a happy husband. And for me," she raised the hem of her şalvar to show off a dazzling pair with a woman, her hands on her hips, worked into the band at the top. "You have a kilim," Ashil said. "Is it for sleeping?"

"My kilim is what we call a quilt. We just use them for cover." She jumped up. "I'll be back." Maggie returned with the quilt. She unfolded it for Ashil.

Ashil looked at each square and saw the placement and pattern throughout. "What does it say?"

Maggie pointed to a yellow square with faded pink roses, "This is an old square of my pajamas, this blue one is a blouse I had and this black one is my old best skirt." She turned away for a moment to collect her thoughts. There was so much of her in the quilt.

Ashil leaned over and studied it carefully. "This kilim is pieces of your life. You can read it." She looked at Maggie. "It's like our carpets, in a way." She handed Maggie the five knitting needles again. "And now you knit a sock."

Maggie picked the needles up slowly. "Anything else I could try?" Maggie had tried knitting before. There were some things, she truly believed, that a person was pre-programmed before birth to fail at—a way to keep humans humble.

"No," Ashil replied.

Four hens clucked contentedly in the yard. Three young boys raced by on the road, laughing at a dog that playfully nipped at their heels. The sun's angle moved over the house, and the shade on the porch shrank to nothingness.

They heard a truck stop and saw Enver and Ali deep in

conversation. Maggie kept her head bent to the wool in her lap. Ali headed toward the village and Enver walked over to the shade of the almond tree.

He avoided Maggie's eyes and looked at the pile of dingy wool that had been mangled to death by the needles. "How's the knitting going?"

"Well enough." Maggie could feel the heat rising from beneath the shapeless top she had thrown over her undershirt. This was the first time he had spoken to her since she had met the chief.

"She's just starting a sock," Ashil volunteered.

"Did you know that socks are used for courting?" He bent over to inspect the sad mess in Maggie's lap. "You won't find a husband with that."

Maggie closed her eyes and slapped him in slow motion movie scene. She opened her eyes and said, "I had a husband. I'm not looking for another one."

A shepherd shouted something to Enver from the road. He glanced down once more at the wool in her lap, and shrugged. "As you say in America, good luck with that." He left without a backward glance.

Maggie studied the pathetic pile of wool in disgust. The sun was warm, too warm. She felt an internal flush of heat, and fanned herself with her hand.

"It's not so good, and not a sock," Ashil pointed to Maggie's pile of wool.

"No. It isn't." Maggie sat back as the flush receded and watched the small brown hens peck the ground.

Maggie sat under the tree in Ashil's yard, folding warm clothes that had dried stiff in the sun. The hens clucked contentedly around her, searching the ground for a tasty morsel. The beekeeper walked by with his buckets of honey, and a young shepherd drove a small herd of sheep past on the road, leaving small puffs of dust in their wake. Neither Ashil nor Ali had returned from their day's business. Maggie had not been invited to go. She rocked back and forth on an old piece of carpet. She heard the crunch of footsteps and saw Enver, tool box in his hand.

"I'm here to work on Ali's truck." He shifted the tool box to his other hand. "Did you see the carpets yesterday?"

"Yes." Maggie held a pile of sparkling white socks in her arm.

"Tell me about them." He set the tool box on the ground beneath the tree, and squatted down next to it. He pulled out a cigarette and struck a match to the bottom of his shoe.

Maggie tucked the socks into the cotton bag and twisted the top together. She didn't know where to begin.

"So, you saw Hala's carpets yesterday?" He asked again.

"No, Ashil showed me Tamay's and Zeynep's and—"

He stood up and shifted the tool box to the porch. "Come with me." Impatience filled his voice. "Come."

Maggie ran slightly to keep up. They walked back through the village to the opposite end, and came to a small stone house. An empty tin bucket was turned bottom side up nearby.

He opened the door to the house. "Come in, I want to show you something." He stationed himself in front of a large carpet hanging on the wall of the single large room. "This is an old carpet Hala made when she was a young woman. I'm going to read it to you."

Maggie had never seen a carpet like the one that hung on the wall. It was filled with colors and motifs that seemed to have little uniformity and yet, it bore a sense of timelessness, a rhythm, something she couldn't verbalize. She stepped back to take it all in. "Where's Hala?"

"Collecting roots for carpet dyes. What do you know about reading kilims and carpets?" Enver asked.

"Well, there are three designs common to all tribes. First, the ram's horn for happiness, or if you're thankful for an abundance of anything. Let's see, second, the hair band is for girls who long to get married," Maggie said. "Then, there's the evil eye to protect the tribes from all bad things. Every tribe has their own brand to identify sheep, rugs and anything else they own, you call it a motif." She stopped. "That's about it."

Enver's eyes widened. "That's more than most westerners know." He pointed to a row of deep pink wool amidst the structured weaving. "Look, Hala was getting married, and she was so happy she had to express herself. See this rifle? Her brother went off to war." His hands flew over the burnished wool. "Now here, the colors are no longer green and white with black, they are this red and this blue—a complete change of colors." He glanced at Maggie. "Do you know why?"

"No." Maggie shook her head.

"Because she got married, moved here to us and took on our colors." Enver rubbed his hand along the carpet and stepped back. "See, the ram's horn is here for a very good year of wool, and here, a cradle for the birth of her son." His voice deepened as he told the story of the old carpet. Enver leaned in closer. "Look, black wool. Her father died." His eyes blazed. "Her life is all here, only now, our women don't weave their lives anymore, they weave," he turned on her with fury in his eyes, "*Elvis*!"

Maggie could feel her voice rising to match his. "This is why I'm here! Mr. Beyter's Foundation will buy every carpet woven in this tribe that the women don't use themselves. They don't have to weave poor carpets with bad wool." She studied the carpet, this time as a reader, not a buyer searching for a perfect size or matching colors. The room was hot and Enver too close. She concentrated on the carpet. "What does this mean?" She pointed to a swath that was mostly black, green and white, seemingly at odds in the midst of the reds, cream and blues of her new tribe.

"Hala was angry with everyone for something and she wanted to go back home. She just wove it right into the rug."

"Did she hang this one out for anyone to see?" Maggie asked.

"Of course, everyone could see it. She said anything she wanted to say in her weaving," Enver said.

"I thought I had to prove myself to the chief before I could learn to read these," Maggie said.

"You do, but I had to show you this one." Enver spoke rapidly. "Tourists want carpets and kilims woven to match some sofas or chairs. They want to pay our women a pittance and sell them for lots of money. They don't care about our history." His face darkened. "This is why I despise the West. And now the women only talk about the carpets they weave for the markets in Antalya that get sent to Istanbul and everywhere else." A fine line of perspiration lined his upper lip, and a deep bitterness crept into his voice. "Our tribe's history is written here," he shook the carpet, "everything. And we're losing it."

"Did you hear what I said?" Maggie asked. "It doesn't have to be that way." Maggie reached out hesitantly to touch the burnished wool.

"Go ahead, touch it." Enver slumped against the wall. "It'll last longer than any of us." A weariness crossed Enver's face. "I have to move a flock of sheep. Go back to Ashil's and tell Ali I'll fix his truck later."

Chapter Six

Maggie walked quickly back to Ashil's. Was reading Hala's carpet some sort of test that Enver was giving her? She had known there would be a series of little tests; she had been tested for her knowledge on every previous project; but here, if she didn't pass each and every one, she could be sent back to Antalya before she had a chance to get to the yayla.

Maggie stood under the tree to collect herself. The hens were clucking and that meant eggs needed to be gathered—later. Enver's heated outburst kept replaying in her head. He wanted the same things that she was here for and yet he didn't talk to the women about it. Why was that so hard to do?

She glanced up at the water tank on the roof. The sun heated the water, and it flowed, gravity fed into the house below. It was a simple device that had changed the lives of the nomads forever. Someone, and not a nomad, had conceived that idea, and convinced this group of people to use it. It could not have been easy.

☙

"Progress is never easy," Mr. Beyter said to Maggie one day as he prepared a speech on artificial insemination of cattle for a group of farmers near Samsun. "But the struggle is worth it."

She had, at that time, worked for him for five years; marveled at his infinite patience with his people and with business men who wanted to move too quickly with changing the nomadic way of life.

"Life has to change, for everyone, not even my people are exempt." He took a tissue and rubbed his glasses, held them up to the light and rubbed one spot again. "In the old days we exchanged rugs and kilims for copper pots, saddles and anything else we needed. Now we sell our goods instead of barter, and the government has limited the areas we can roam. But—a people should always preserve that part of themselves which makes them unique." He smiled kindly over the rim of his glasses. "Our women have woven the language of our history into our carpets since ancient times. There is a way to preserve that past, but," he sighed, "change for all of us is sometimes slow and difficult."

෴

A sudden breeze brought Maggie back to her task at hand. The eggs still resting in brown straw were to be a part of the evening meal. She stepped into the hen house and picked up six brown ones, placed them into her apron, held the ends of the apron together and walked back to the kitchen.

Ashil had returned from her business in the village. She took the eggs from Maggie and set them on a soft cloth near a wooden bowl of walnut pieces. She lifted the lid on a Dutch oven and stirred something that caused Maggie's mouth to water.

Ashil wiped water off a copper pot. "We'll have those eggs tonight with some walnuts, and yogurt soup."

They worked in companionable silence. Maggie rolled dough to bake the bread, and Ashil strained milk for yogurt until the sun sank behind the mountains and Ali returned from his day with the goats. They ate the simple meal and washed it down with glasses of steaming tea.

Ali spoke to Ashil of the day's work, of the crops of grain other village members tilled, and of the upcoming trip to the yayla. Maggie listened, it was harder to understand Ali than Ashil, but over time she had gotten accustomed to his manner of speech.

Ashil poured the last of the tea into their glasses. "Maggie made the bread tonight, and this is her first time to make the tea."

"The bread tastes like it should, but the tea," Ali swallowed the last bit, "is not so good." He lit a cigarette. Maggie sat quietly. That was the first time Ali had directed a single comment to her. She had made bread from a thousand year old recipe and pleased one nomad man—one tiny success, hooray.

Several men arrived later and gathered on the porch to talk and smoke. Ashil took a bottle of raki and glasses out to them. "We're going to Hala's," she said to Ali and shooed the chickens away from the porch.

Maggie, armed awkwardly with a ball of wool on her arm and a wooden hand spindle she would have to learn to use, listened as Ashil hummed on the dusty road to Hala's. What if she couldn't learn all of this? The knot in the pit of her stomach had loosened, but stayed there, ready to whorl itself into a heavy tangle at a moment's notice. She hoped it would not remain in residence throughout the summer.

As they neared Hala's house, several women joined them. They carried babies in colorful bags on their backs. Scorpions adorned each bag. These motifs kept danger at bay, the women said. By weaving a scorpion motif into a baby's blanket, the women had power over and protection from a real scorpion. The mothers gently scolded young children who played hide and seek around their legs, darting into the voluminous folds of their şalvars.

Laughter. She heard it everywhere—and singing. They passed a group of men, sitting on the steps of a house, smoking and drinking raki. Four of them sang in rich deep voices of yaylas of sweet grass, fat sheep and good wool.

Hala sat in front of her small stone house. She had a large wooden vertical loom set up in the middle of the front porch, and two other women had portable horizontal looms at each end. A passage way to the door was the only space not crawling with women and their small children.

Hala came close to Maggie and peered up into her eyes. "Welcome. Do you weave?"

"Not yet," Maggie said.

"Let me see your hands," Hala commanded.

Maggie held out her hands, and Hala rubbed her fingers. "Are they nimble like the lambs?"

Maggie strained to understand her words. "Beg your pardon?"

"Can you tie a knot? Are your hands too old to tie a good knot?" Hala muttered to herself and shook her head. "I'm sure they are."

"I'd like to try." Maggie knew the difference between Turkish and Persian knots. Reading about them and examining them with Omar in his carpet shop was a long way from tying them on a wooden loom in the company of master weavers.

"Sema, would you bring us tea?" Hala nodded toward the şamovar in the corner. She then turned to a young girl in the group. "Show Maggie Hanim nimble fingers and what you can do with them."

The shy young girl sat down at the loom, where roughly a third of a carpet was complete. The colors were magnificent. Balls of blue, burgundy, cream, green, and brown wool hung at the top of the loom, and the young girl began tying knots with a swiftness and mastery Maggie could only admire.

Throughout the entire carpet, there often was a single strand of wool knotted and hanging down. Maggie knew that each woman that visited Hala would take a few minutes and weave a row or two. Each one would leave one telltale thread as a sign of her visit and her weaving. The number of threads was a testament to all the women who came and sat in the presence of this tribal elder.

"This carpet," Hala sipped on the glass of amber tea Sema placed in her hand, "will be finished when the almonds from that tree have turned brown."

There were between 25 and 600 knots per square inch in these types of Turkish carpets, Maggie had read. She had studied enough with Omar to tell that this stunning carpet was on the high end.

"It's a beautiful piece." Maggie was overwhelmed with the craftsmanship and time commitment before her. She studied the group of women and girls. All except the youngest were turning hand spindles as they talked and laughed.

Surely now was the time to tell them all about Mr. Beyter's offer to buy their carpets. It would be good to do it in a group. A niggling fear caused her to refrain. The chief hadn't given her permission yet and he was the sole person who could stop her from making this trip.

Sema brought tea, and every woman present told her of an item they were weaving, embroidering or knitting for her daughter Leslihan. Sema beamed in the limelight and showed her prowess on the rows of perfect knots she tied on Hala's carpet.

The women laughed and played with their children. They drank tea and spun their wool. Maggie drifted away, into an English conversation with Haluk and Lahli. She was in Antalya having dinner in Old Town, wearing a black linen dress and drinking chardonnay with the two of them, Haluk teasing her and Lahli teasing them both. She missed it, all of it. What she wouldn't give for a long hot shower and a feather bed, the silkiness of moist air from the Mediterranean and Haluk bantering with her over a succulent dinner.

Hala coughed and Maggie's mind flitted back to her tea.

Picking her teeth, Hala surveyed the group as the evening faded into early twilight. "So, who is going to wash wool tomorrow?" There was some faint mumbling.

Ashil spoke quickly, "I will. I have mallets, and Maggie Hanim can work with me."

Tamay un-wrapped a child from her leg, "I'll rinse."

Sema spoke through a loud yawn, "I'll lay it to dry and separate it, but I can't comb."

Hala caught the yawn. "I'll comb." She got up and moved toward the door. With the unspoken dismissal, some of the women collected the tea glasses and disappeared into the house; others gathered up children and started toward their homes.

Ashil and Maggie walked slowly back along the road that had grown silent. A full moon bathed the road in silver light.

"We have to have the wool ready before we go to the yayla." Ashil smiled at Maggie as they entered the house. "Have a good sleep. Today was not so busy, but tomorrow we will work hard and long."

☙

Ashil was right. For four days Maggie had pounded burlap bags filled with new wool with a heavy wooden mallet. This loosened the dirt that clung to it. Maggie pulled her scarf up over her nose when a pungent smell wafted out of a bag. She kept up a steady rhythm. She had been smart and put her compression sleeve on before she started working. She couldn't afford to look weak—people who were considered weak were often ignored.

Small children and teen-aged girls gathered the wool up and carried it to flat places near the village well. There it was rinsed carefully by Tamay, who spouted directions to a different brood of village children. Other women and children carried it to flat rocks on the edge of the village square and stretched it out to dry in the afternoon sun.

Maggie leaned against a tree, massaging her arm. She was exhausted. She smelled like wet wool. The village center was a hive of activity. Everyone, down to the smallest child was involved in preparation for the months they would spend high in the mountains she could see from her window every day.

She saw Enver standing on the other side of the well among several young herdsmen. A tiny boy was crawling up his leg, and another one pulled on his arm. He removed them without a break in the conversation, and they ran back to their mothers.

She had seen him around the village, talking with the men and smoking with the chief. He was her only connection to any kind of life other than this, and he wouldn't even have a conversation with her, give her a chance to speak English for a moment. When he did talk to her he made fun of her knitting. A pox on him. Really.

Enver noticed her and ambled over when the herdsmen had left him. She involuntarily reached to pat her headscarf back into place.

"This is much harder than life in Antalya, isn't it?" He didn't wait for an answer. "Tell Ashil to take you around to see the old carpets the women have."

"Not now." She pointed to the pile of wet smelly wool. "As you can't help but see, we're very busy."

"I see that. Do what I tell you." He took a quick pull on his cigarette. "Ashil is a good woman because she listens to Ali. You would do good to pay attention."

Maggie picked up the mallet and smashed it into the wool two inches from Enver's foot.

"Watch what you're doing!" He jumped away.

"*You* would do good to pay attention." She hit the ground again, and water splashed onto his shoe. He swore at her, she was sure, and hefted a bag of heavy wet wool over his shoulder. He stalked over to Tamay and dropped it near her feet without a word.

Tamay looked up at him and then at Maggie in surprise. Carrying wool was a woman's job.

At the moment Maggie didn't care whose job was what. All she wanted to do was to sit, drink a cup of coffee and eat enough aspirin to make the pounding in her head and arm slow down to match the pounding of her mallet on the wool.

೧

Maggie was satisfied with her pace of acceptance. After three weeks of hard work, she had found a place with the women. Her bread making, knowledge of the kovan when churning butter and her diligent work with the wool had earned her some tribal respect.

In conversations, over tea and daily chores, first Ashil, and then the other women had asked Maggie about her life in Antalya. She had tried to tell them, but without a reference in their own lives, they soon tired of her attempts to convey it in a way they could understand. She talked to them instead about Mr. Beyter, his desire to see that their handwork and carpets fetched the best price at the market.

"Will you talk to us about selling our rugs before we go to the yayla?" Ashil had asked the question one afternoon. "We'd like to know how to get a better price."

"Of course." Maggie was delighted to be asked. It was a milestone in her quest to get to know the women better.

Ashil gathered the women in the early afternoon before the evening meal. Maggie sat on an old carpet. She leaned against Ali's worn camel saddle, festooned with braids of new wool. It was breezy and a fire lapped lazily at the pile of wood in the cooking pit. Not to waste a bit of heat, lamb stew simmered in several pots.

Maggie was moved by the expectant faces gathered around her. "Thanks for coming. Ashil said you wanted to talk about how to deal with people when you go down to the market in Manavgat."

One of the women held up an exquisite head covering, complete with embroidered dangles. Another offered up a handkerchief of fine transparent cotton. Laid out at their feet were months of weaving small prayer carpets, camel covers, donkey saddle covers and water bags.

Maggie stood in front of the women. "First, I'm going to pretend to be a buyer, and then I'll pretend to be Ashil." Maggie played both parts in the role-playing exercise, and laughed with them as they began to understand.

She grinned at Ashil and Sema. "Now you two can do it. Ashil, you can be a fat man with a lot of money," Maggie suggested. "Come here to buy this rug from Sema. You want it very badly."

Shy at first, and with a few hesitant starts, they soon became comfortable with the idea.

The women lost themselves in the roles with Maggie providing only a little encouragement. The other women laughed and clapped as Ashil deepened her voice and made big gestures.

"Do I have to offer to make the fat man tea?" Sema laughed at Ashil, who had swaggered over to the carpet.

"Get your wife to do it, Sema," Zeynep giggled behind her hand.

"And get her to make me some too. I want to be the man," Tamay said.

The women each took a turn at bartering for the carpet. Sema put her finger under her nose and made a moustache. "I'm hungry, and I want a sweet cake, and you must obey because I am a man." She pointed to Ashil who burst into laughter.

They didn't notice Enver and two other men until they came around the edge of the house. Maggie caught a word or two about the size of the sheep herds and something about fuel for the trucks. All but Enver ignored the women, and walked past on their way for an evening smoke at the tent.

"There's a lot of laughing going on here," Enver said tightly. "What are you doing?"

"Learning how to deal with Westerners," Maggie said truthfully. None of the other women spoke.

"You were told by the chief and me that you couldn't do this until he said you could." The steeliness in his voice matched the hardness of his eyes. "Do you want to go back to Antalya?" Enver cupped his hand under Maggie's elbow and steered her to a spot out of hearing of the other women. "If you do this again, you very well may not be going to the yayla at all. Is that what Mr. Beyter wanted?"

A hot flush rose to Maggie's cheeks. "Don't you dare talk to me about what Mr. Beyter wanted."

"Someone has to," Enver said. "What you want is absolutely not important. What *is* important is that you obey the rules of this tribe and its leader." His grip on her elbow tightened. "I brought you here and I can take you back."

They both turned as they heard the women behind them. Sema had commandeered a rock and was spouting directions to the other women who dissolved into helpless laughter.

"I didn't volunteer to talk to them about this, they asked me." Maggie shook off his hand. "I'm leaving."

Chapter Seven

THE RUMBLE OF thunder faded. The sun peeked out occasionally through the last of the clouds that danced across the sky on their way toward the mountains. The rain shower had left the air moist, and Maggie tilted her nose to draw in the scent of damp earth. She poured the collected rain water into the wash tubs.

Ashil appeared at the top of the stairs with a basket of dirty clothes. She dropped it in the corner and leaned against one of the legs to the water tank. "It smells good. I like the rain."

"When I was growing up the rain meant we could stop working the fields, stop picking cotton for a few minutes," Maggie said.

"A chance to rest," Ashil nodded. "What else did you grow on your land?"

"We didn't own the land. Some men owned many hectares, we call them acres. They grew cotton mostly, but some of them planted fruit trees—.

"Like figs or olives?" Ashil asked.

"Some figs, no olives, some peaches." Maggie's thoughts flew to ladders and bushel baskets of fruit, bees and stifling heat. But the worst by far, the soul killer, was the sun baking her bent head as she pulled puffy white cotton from sharp pronged bolls and stuffed it into a heavy sack looped over a shoulder. Her back and shoulders ached from dragging a sack down dusty rows to the mesh sided wagon that held the cotton and the scales. An overseer hung the bag on the scales, penciled in the weight and multiplied that by eight cents a pound. He wrote it down on a pad and Maggie trudged back into the endless field. At days end she collected her daily wage. On the day Maggie turned thirteen she waited with the others at quitting time. The overseer lifted her bag to the scales, added the number to her previous ones for the day and handed it to Maggie. She didn't hear him tell her how much she had earned. She just stared at the numbers. She had picked her weight in cotton. All her future accomplishments would be measured against that hot autumn day.

Maggie knew Mr. Beyter appreciated her grit. He had told her so. They both agreed that one did what one must to survive, and they were both the stronger for it.

Maggie snapped back to the present. She looked at the basket of clothes, "More washing?"

"No, Maggie Hanim, today it's your turn to milk," Ashil said.

Maggie dried her hands on her apron. "I wondered when my turn would come. I'm ready and glad it has nothing to do with wool."

In the time she had been in the village, Maggie had washed wool, rinsed wool, dried wool, combed wool, dreamt wool, and finally all of it, every last curly piece of it had been stuffed

Stone the Goat

into sacks and readied for the trip to the yayla.

"Let's go." Ashil handed Maggie four buckets, and picked up four. "This is important today, and we're happy for you."

"We who?" Maggie opened the door to see Tamay, Sema, Zeynep and many of the children in a line spiraling its way behind the chicken coop. "An audience?"

"Yes," Ashil was excited, "they just want to see an American milk our goats."

"Okay." Maggie grinned at them all. "Let's go."

Maggie entered first, and scanned the corral. She released a long sigh when the giant ram was nowhere in sight. She made her way to a flat surface, devoid of manure, and sat down cross legged on the ground. "Bring me a goat."

Four women simultaneously walked toward her with a handful of grain and a ewe to milk. The children squatted down near her and chattered away.

"One at a time, please. Ashil, Sema, Zeynep and Tamay." Maggie wrapped her arms around the back end of the first ewe and pulled it close enough to lean forward and find the udders. With her head turned to keep her nose out of its newly shorn butt, she gave a gentle pull to the swollen teats. With a practiced hand she started the steady flow into the tin bucket. It hit the bottom in an urgent splash. Some of the milk ran over Maggie's fingers, and the warm drops felt good on her hand. After a few minutes she palpated the udder to make sure she was leaving some for the kids, and then patted the goat on the rump.

"Next." Maggie flashed a smile at Ashil.

The women murmured their approval as Maggie quickly milked the small herd. Soon, bored with her efficiency, they wandered off back toward the village. The children had left long ago.

"You have milked before, I think," Ashil said as Maggie dusted her apron off. "Enver never said you could milk. He said you didn't know our lives, Maggie, and you were spoiled to softness, like bad eggs."

"Really?" Maggie wiped her face with her sleeve and stopped mid wipe. Ashil had used her first name only. Maggie raised her head to see a hint of acceptance in Ashil's eyes. Her heart sang. She wiped her face once more. "Enver doesn't know anything about me. I think you should decide on your own."

☙

The sun was warm and the air still when someone darkened the doorway of Ashil's cooking hut.

"Hello." Enver squatted down next to Maggie at the bread board. He picked up a piece of hot yufka. "May I have one?"

Maggie kept her eyes on the rolling pin as she made slow methodic movements over the dough. "If you need to ask, ask Ashil."

"We're leaving in a week." He tore off a bite size piece and offered it to her.

"No thanks." Maggie ignored the bit of food.

"Talk to me," Enver said.

"Why?" Maggie sat back on her heels. "You ignore me and

make fun of my knitting." She mashed the handful of dough until it squirted between her fingertips. "You seem to think the women here are the only ones in the world who know how to work hard."

He frowned. "Our women do work harder than western women."

"And how many western women do you know? Only city women? London, didn't you go to school there, or some from New York, or Paris?" She snorted. "Soft as eggs. You are so wrong."

"I'm not wrong, but I never argue with women." Enver finished eating the yufka and picked up another one. "If you had a chance to go back to Antalya, would you go?" There was a sense of urgency in his question.

"What are you talking about?" Maggie blew hair out of her eyes.

The muscle in Enver's jaw tightened. "For once, would you just answer a question with a yes or no."

"Well ..." Maggie pushed her hair behind her ear. "No, I wouldn't go back, not yet. I haven't been to the yay—"

"Maggie, are you in there?" Puzzled, Maggie turned to Enver but heard Haluk's voice speaking in English. A moment later, Haluk stuck his head into the door of the hut. "Alive, are you?" He grinned, "All sweaty and covered with enough flour to make another big yufka."

Maggie scrambled to her feet and steeled herself from launching directly into his arms. She wanted to bury her face in the linen jacket he was wearing. "I'm so happy to see you," she said.

Haluk pulled her to him and kissed both cheeks. "A proper welcome." He stepped back, still holding her hands. "That was a hello from Dr. Lahli as well."

A discreet cough separated them. Haluk released Maggie's hands and pushed his sunglasses up into his hair. "Hello. Did you see how our Maggie welcomed me? You're not working her too hard, are you?"

"Yes, I saw how she welcomed you," Enver said. "If we're working her too hard she can go back to Antalya with you." Enver looked over Maggie's head to Haluk. "Perhaps she's had all the nomad life she can endure."

"Whose donkey kicked you?" Haluk laughed. "She's tough. She'll come down from the yayla with all of the women wanting her to stay forever."

"Don't think that's going to happen." Maggie wiped flour from her hands.

"When you've finished greeting your American friend, the men want to see you. We've got to get those samples." Enver stepped out of the hut and disappeared around the house.

"It's so good to see you." Maggie shivered with happiness. "Why are you here?"

"Dr. Lahli asked me to get some samples from the sheep for some blood testing before they go to the yayla. There's a strain of some disease that seems to be popping up in our region."

"Goats, too?" Maggie asked. "I just milked the herd yesterday."

Stone the Goat

"Just grazing sheep, and before you interrupted—I was going to say, I'm here to get those for her and to see you before you leave. She asked, I said yes." Haluk caressed her with his eyes. "You look pale and you smell so ..." He wrinkled his nose slightly and pushed the headscarf down and ruffled her hair. "I'm off to get samples for her and I'll see you tonight."

"How long are you staying?" Maggie didn't want him to leave.

"I have to go back in the morning." He stepped out of the hut, ran his fingers through his mane of hair and sighed. "The things I do for the women in my life."

Throughout the afternoon, a lavish communal meal was prepared in honor of Haluk's arrival and Lahli's willingness to always keep track of the health of the herds. She knew that a tribe could be devastated by the loss of their livelihood. Lalhi had been gone from the tribe for years, but her heart remained in the village of her people. Not every tribe had such connections.

At dusk, the men swallowed Haluk up in their raki drinking, cigarette smoking, and heavy cloud of testosterone. From across the fire, Maggie studied the differences in Enver and Haluk as they ate and drank. Haluk was amiable but out of place in his wrinkled shirt and expensive trousers. He said something that caused the men to laugh. Enver smoked quietly and listened as Haluk held court. He rarely joined in the conversation.

Maggie chafed at the cultural constraints which dictated she stay with the women. She wanted some time to be with

Haluk, to catch up on Omar and his carpets, to see what Kemal and the waiters were doing at the hotel; and most of all, to have him tell her Lahli and Florence were missing her.

Instead she was listening as they talked yet again about the yayla, the wedding and who was weaving what and for whom.

Later, Haluk walked over to Maggie at the end of the meal. He smelled of smoke, raki and the familiar fragrance of his almond soap.

"Want to come back with me?" Haluk asked. His hair gleamed in the firelight.

"Want a donkey and a goat in your condo?" Maggie hoped he didn't press her to go back. Today she wasn't the strong woman she thought herself to be. She was tired enough to just get into the car and go. Back to hot water, long baths, and civilization, back to a change in their relationship, perhaps.

"I forgot," he smiled at her and shook his head, "you can't come back yet. I'll see you in the morning before I go."

୧୨

The camp hummed with anticipation. Three days and they would be on the trek to a higher ground. Haluk had gone back to Antalya, and Maggie had pretended to be asleep when he called for her at her door flap the morning he left. It was safer that way. Less tempting to just grab her bags and slide into the company car.

In the weeks since her arrival Maggie had milked under the watchful eye of Ashil twice a day. She had developed a row of calluses across the palms of both hands, learned where

Stone the Goat

to store the milk for yogurt, how to churn butter and how to make çökelek, a dried yogurt staple to be used on the trip to the yayla. It was time to lose the training wheels.

Maggie adjusted her scarf. "May I go alone today? I can do this, you know."

Ashil tied a knot at her loom. "You're right. You can go but don't start milking until the others get there. Come back as soon as you're finished." Ashil surveyed the pearl gray morning sky. "You may be the earliest one there."

Maggie gathered up the buckets and stepped outside. She glanced at the first signs of sunlight on the mountain peaks. "If no one's there, I'll wait." She stopped to pick a handful of green almonds from the tree at the porch, and dropped all but one into her apron pocket. She popped it into her mouth and bit down—the crunch was satisfying.

It was good to be away from the perpetual scrutiny of life in the village. What she craved was some time alone—and more than that, a dark chocolate bar of any kind.

Ashil was correct in her prediction, Maggie noted. Signs of life had not appeared from any of the other chimneys.

Maggie reached the corral and scanned the enclosure, happy to see the big breeding ram wasn't there. The ewes were restless, heavy with milk, and the kids fretted in the small shed. She hesitated for a moment. She could slip in and get the other buckets from the shed, and have them ready when the women arrived. She stepped inside, hung the buckets on one arm and fumbled with the latch. She froze when a forceful nudge pushed her past the gate. The giant ram had appeared from behind the shed and was sniffing her butt.

"Get away! Go on!" She frowned at the ram and slapped him on his hindquarters as Ashil had done. He whirled with an angry snort, lowered his head and slammed into her, trapping her just out of reach of the gate.

"Get out of here!" Maggie threw the buckets at him. He grazed her arm with a wild shake of his head. She scrambled for a jagged rock and threw it with all her might. She heard it crack against his skull and saw the blood spurt from his eye. The ram bellowed in rage and the twisted point of his left horn ripped into Maggie's şalvar. Frantic, she closed her hand over two rough stones and shrieked when he whirled around and slashed into her just beneath her outstretched arm. Wild with rage, the ram snorted, pawed his bleeding eye and lowered his horns like a mad bull. Maggie screamed and slung a stone.

"Stop it!" Hands shot around her waist and lifted her into the air. She aimed the last stone and let it fly.

"I said stop it!" Enver shook her. "That's our best ram and you're killing him!" He set her writhing body down with a thump. "He gored you. I saw it. Turn around."

"If he comes close to me again, I'll kill him," Maggie trembled violently. She wrapped her arms tightly around herself.

"You will not. Are you bleeding?" Enver asked.

"I damn sure will, and no I'm not." Maggie struggled to control her trembling.

Enver left Maggie long enough to grab the ram by his horns and drag him a few feet away. She could see the blood spilling over the animal's eye. Enver quickly took his turban and bound the head of the ram, pushed it into a small stall inside the corral and walked swiftly back to her.

"This ram," Enver said, his black eyes sparking rage "may lose his eye because of you."

"He attacked me." Maggie's breath was still ragged.

"Show me where he gored you," Enver said.

Maggie held out her hands. Her pale skin was scraped and raw, a dark red spot grew where a bruise would be soon.

"No, where he gored you, I saw him." Enver stepped closer.

"My skirt." Maggie held up the ripped skirt and vest.

"I saw him. You screamed." Enver's breath was on her hair, "What's wrong with your blouse?"

"Nothing!" Maggie clamped her arms closer together and spun away. "Leave me alone! Why are you here?"

"Because someone has to watch out for you. Let me see your blouse." Enver caught up with Maggie as she reached the gate. He twirled her around to face him. "I will not have you here sick with infection. Show me or I'll send you back to Antalya." He shook her shoulders. "Show me."

"Show you?" Maggie yanked her blouse open and buttons flew. She peeled it off and threw it at Enver's feet. She stripped off her bra and slung it at him. It landed with a thud at his feet. Enver's eyes locked on her exposed chest. Maggie watched him shift his gaze from one firm white breast to the flattened chest and the long white scar.

"That damned ram didn't hurt me, he gored my breast." Maggie stooped down, picked up her blouse and crushed it against her chest. "Did you see enough? Pick up my bra and give it to me."

Enver stood unmoving.

Maggie stepped forward and picked up the bra. She stood upright and lifted her chin. "Go away. I have goats to milk."

She turned and stumbled to the shed. She examined the bra and saw the large jagged hole gouged out of the bra and the prosthetic breast. She left the damaged breast inside the bra, fastened it once more and tied her blouse back together at the waist.

Outside, Maggie took a deep breath, lifted the legs of her şalvar and sat down in the midst of the milling goats. There was no one to bring a ewe to her. She wrapped her arms around her knees and rocked. One tiny sob escaped.

The rattle of grain on a metal plate startled her. Enver moved toward her with a ewe in tow.

Maggie searched his inscrutable eyes. She took a breath, wiped her nose on her sleeve and yanked the hind end of the smelly goat toward her. She placed a practiced hand on the warm udder, and laid her wet cheek on the dirty wool. *Oh, Robert.*

∽

Maggie stood at the kitchen door window and stared at two cardinals perched on the bird feeder. She felt Robert's chin on her head. "What should I do?"

"I don't know babe. I really don't know. What do you want to do?" Robert asked.

Stone the Goat

"Have my boob back," Maggie said.

"Me too." He ran his fingers down her shoulder and rested the palm of his hand on the new scar. "I can feel your heartbeat. Never felt it like that before."

Maggie laid her hand on top of his. She felt life coursing through her body in every steady thump. "I can feel it too. It's strong."

Robert turned her around to face him. "Like you."

"Can you stand a one breasted woman?" Maggie held her breath.

"Only if she lets me feel her heartbeat," Robert said, pulling her close.

☙

Enver stayed with Maggie and wordlessly brought her goats until the first of the women showed up to milk. He left quickly, put a rope around the ram's neck and led it into the woods behind the corral. The women chattered among themselves, unaware of the catastrophe of Maggie's doing. They finished milking and divided the bounty. Maggie carried her buckets back to Ashil's, numb to the pain in her palms. A sense of impending doom enveloped her. No one was at the house when she arrived. She poured the milk into the tin pails and fled to her room to more carefully inspect the damage to her bra and breast.

It was worse than she had thought. The horn had gouged a large hole three inches deep into the soft material of the prosthesis. Another half inch and the ram's horn would have ripped her chest wall open. She couldn't think about this now.

Maggie tightly closed the entire ordeal off to deal with later. She had learned to compartmentalize as a child. It had saved her.

The chores would not wait for her to decide what to do. Maggie trudged dutifully to the back step and started churning the butter.

Soon Ashil stuck her head out the back door, "Breakfast?"

"No," Maggie said. "I'm not hungry."

In a few minutes Ashil stuck her head out the door again, "Enver is here to see you, were you expecting him?"

"Absolutely," Maggie said evenly. She patted the butter dry.

She hadn't known whether to tell Ashil or not. She needed to talk to Enver, to explain. Now he was out front waiting for her.

"Are you going to see the chief?" Ashil asked. "Here's some eggs for him."

"I'm pretty sure I am," Maggie said.

Maggie touched her head. She imprisoned several errant strands of hair under her headscarf and pulled it back into position. Resigned to her probable fate, she picked up the basket of eggs and walked around the house to see Enver standing at the edge of the porch.

He took a short fast draw on a cigarette. "There you are." He stepped off the porch and flipped the butt on the ground. "The chief is waiting."

When they arrived, it took a moment for Maggie to realize that there were no villagers in the square, no children laughing at the well. There had been no one on the road, and no men stood at the door to the big black tent.

"Follow me." Enver raised the flap.

Maggie's eyes adjusted quickly to the interior. The inside was very light, the goat hair filtered light well. The ground was covered in large thick carpets, the tribal colors of indigo and deep red prominent throughout. A large copper pot for tea sat steaming in one corner, and pillows were piled in all four corners. The chief sat cross-legged in the middle, without the customary glass of tea in his hand.

"Sit there." He motioned Maggie to a place in front of him. Enver sat next to him, on the right, facing Maggie. The tent flap opened and Ashil's husband Ali entered. He sat down on the chief's left side.

Maggie was not offered a glass of tea, a testament to her unwelcome presence. She sank to her knees, unwilling to go further.

The chief started without preamble. "You stoned our breeding ram today. Why?"

"He attacked me," Maggie said.

"You have a strange smell. It's rutting season and he was protecting his ewes. Now he could lose his eye," the chief said.

Maggie protested in a low voice, "I didn't do anything wrong." She felt perspiration forming on her skin, sliding down her back to safety. Even her sweat was abandoning her. She reached to wipe her smoke irritated eyes and stopped. No one was going to say she had cried.

"Yes, you did do something wrong." The chief pointed

his finger at Maggie. "You told Ashil you would wait for the women, and you didn't." He wagged his finger in her face. "I've been told you don't have a single mark on you."

Maggie's eyes flew toward Enver. "I did tell Ashil I would wait, but I didn't think it was wrong to go inside the corral and get the buckets ready."

"If you don't know what you are doing, don't do it." He turned to Enver. "You brought this woman here and expect us to take her to the yayla. Control her. If she makes trouble again, you will send her back to Haluk. Our promise to Mustafa Beyter ends."

Maggie rose to her feet and stood over the men, still seated cross legged on the floor.

"You're not dismissed." The chief glowered. He blew smoke up toward Maggie's face. "Sit down."

She saw Ali and Enver's eyes rivet on the chief.

"No," Maggie said.

"My legacy depends on you ... "

Mr. Beyter's words rang in her ears.

"No, I won't sit down," Maggie trembled in a rage she barely contained. "You are not going to send me back to anyone."

"Maggie," Enver said and started to rise. "You need ..."

"Sit." She shot him a withering glance. "I'm not finished." She had heard enough. "I came to this tribe, to this place, for Mr. Beyter. I've done everything you've ordered Ashil to have me to do. Everything. I've respected your culture, respect mine."

"Maggie," Enver warned.

Maggie lowered her face to the chief and spoke clearly. "I don't belong to Enver, to Haluk or to anyone. I belong to myself—don't you ever forget that."

Maggie turned her back on the three men, still sitting in shock from her outburst, lifted the flap and disappeared into the bright morning. Her heart pounded as she walked slowly to Ashil's house. Enver had said nothing in her defense. *Nothing*. Not a single word.

Maggie heard Ashil on the far end of the roof and slipped in through the side entrance to avoid her. In her small room she leaned her head against the closed door and expelled a long breath. Maggie lay down on the pile of sleeping carpets and gazed unseeingly at the ceiling.

༺

Maggie stuck a toothpick through the waxed paper and placed the second sandwich in the stack of food for Robert's lunchbox. "Let's see, apple, sandwiches, two plums, cookies …"

"Don't skimp on cookies. A working man needs lots of cookies." Robert shook crumbs out of an ancient lunchbox and stopped to glance out the kitchen window. "Listen to that wind, doesn't sound good."

"I checked the rain gauge when I started the coffee," Maggie said, "Four inches since we went to bed." Maggie sipped her coffee as Robert carefully wiped the outside of the lunchbox. The black metal was scraped and dented, the handle bound with yards of frayed duct tape, partial stickers spoke to the World War II airplanes and slogans in its long history. It had belonged to his father, and his grandfather before him.

Robert inspected the handle for a moment. "Might need some more duct tape if this thing is going to hold up for another generation." He grinned at her.

"Let's worry about it lasting this generation," Maggie laughed. She took the lunchbox from him, placed the pile of food inside just so and carefully tamped it down. She snapped it shut and turned to him with her face upturned. He kissed her and nuzzled her ear. "We need a strapping son to inherit the Meadows lunchbox." He tickled her thigh.

"Son?" Maggie tapped his chest. "Why a son?"

"It's a manly lunchbox, for a boy, not a lunch purse." He ran a finger down her cheek. "Soon?"

She arched her eyebrows at him. "Very soon."

Thunder rumbled and roared overhead, and a dozen bolts of lightning lit up the sky. Robert released her and reached for the lunchbox and his utility company hardhat. "When this thing passes there'll be lines down everywhere. Another long day," he said. "Love you, kiddo. Call when I can."

"Be careful, Robert. I love you, too." Maggie watched him sprint in the morning downpour to his old beat up Ford pickup. An F150 with one hundred and eighty thousand miles he had told Maggie when they married—and he intended to pass it on. He waved as he backed to the end of the driveway and looked both ways before backing into the street.

Back inside, Maggie glanced at the clock. Mr. Beyter was

Stone the Goat

in Istanbul on business and she could go to the office any time of day. If she waited, this fast moving thunderstorm would be hammering another county in an hour. She could get the laundry going, exercise and shower before going to work. She peered out the window at the rain blowing sideways in gusts along the street she now could barely see.

The doorbell rang just as Maggie checked her hair and did a 360 spin in front of the full length mirror. Perfect timing, she had gotten everything done. She slipped into her shoes and headed for the door. The thunder storm had moved eastward and the rain had tapered off to a steady but gentle shower. Who would be out so soon?

She opened it to find two Oklahoma Highway Patrolmen standing before her. Both were friends of Robert's, college classmates, baseball teammates and fishing buddies. Water sluiced from their hats and dripped from their eyes as they stepped inside and told her. A drunk driver had crossed the center line driving on the wrong side of the two lane highway. He surfaced from a low spot in the road. Robert swerved to avoid him. He and the old F150 had no chance. The drunk man walked away from the wreck and hid in the ditch. The patrolmen had found him there.

Both men caught Maggie as her knees buckled.

A drunk driver ... sixth offense ... he was so sorry ... hadn't meant to ... if only he could ... the newspapers got it right. Robert Meadows ... on his way to work ... leaves behind loving parents, siblings and a loving wife ... such a tragic loss.

And no children.

There was a sharp knock on the door. "Are you in there?" Ashil asked.

"Yes," Maggie said.

"May I come in?" she asked.

"Yes." Maggie roused and opened the door.

Ashil stepped in with her hand spindle turning furiously. "I heard that the men want you to leave."

"I'm sure they do." Maggie covered her eyes. Her head was exploding.

"They said you stoned the best ram and he can't see and isn't worth anything and that you didn't have any blood on you. Is that true?"

"Yes."

"How can that be? I need to know this." Ashil waited in a din of deafening silence.

"I can't explain this in your language." Maggie slowly unbuttoned her blouse. She pointed to her bra. "Do you wear something like this?"

"Not just so, but yes." Ashil's eyes widened.

Maggie turned, removed her blouse and bra, draped a scarf over her shoulders and turned to face Ashil.

"Here is why the ram didn't draw blood." She held out the carefully mended bra in one hand and the punctured prosthetic breast in the other.

Ashil focused intently on the breast. "I don't understand."

Maggie laid the breast and bra on the small table, and lowered the shawl. For the second time in one day she exposed herself to someone who stared at her chest.

Ashil caught Maggie's eye and an arc of understanding flashed across the barriers of language and cultural divide. She reached for Maggie's hand and they knelt together on the soft carpet. "Show me," Ashil said.

Maggie saw the quizzical frown, the genuine concern that flickered in Ashil's' dark eyes, the white scarf tucked so carefully behind her ears. Maggie took the prosthesis and held it in her hand. "This is made of a material that will get warm like your skin."

"No." Ashil drew back slightly.

"Yes, please." Maggie reached for Ashil's brown hand, placed it on the soft material, and covered it with her own white one. "Wait." In seconds, the prosthesis was warm.

"And so, I just tuck it into this pocket that's made especially for the breast," Maggie said when she could speak, smoothing the front of the cup over the breast beneath. She slipped it on and turned her back to Ashil. She felt Ashil's hands hooking the clasps. For a moment Maggie stood facing the wall, blinded by a deluge of tears she didn't expect and couldn't control. She turned back to Ashil. "This is me now."

Ashil gently adjusted the shawl over Maggie's shoulders, touched her finger to Maggie's cheek, causing a stream of tears to alter its course. "I understand."

Chapter Eight

A WAGON TRAIN of trucks rumbled past Maggie's window and stopped in a single file pointed toward the higher mountains. She heard the goats grunting, chickens squawking, and saw the camels with their long necks hung over the wooden slats of the trailers chewing their cuds. Herdsmen checked the latches one more time.

There were more trucks. Maggie wasn't sure where they all came from. They were stuffed with women and children and piled high with all the goods necessary for a summer high in the mountains. They shuddered under the weight of bags of wool, pots and pans, bags of clothing, feed for chickens and piles of carpets. Drivers shouted last minute instructions to each other. Maggie knew Ashil would come for her when Ali was ready. The best thing she could do was just stay out of the way.

In the three days since she stoned the ram Maggie had quickly faded into the background. She didn't know what Ashil had told the other women. The paramount tribal objective was to get ready for this trip—and here they were.

She heard Ashil call, picked up her two duffel bags and walked to the front door. Ashil and Ali stood by the first of three trucks that belonged to them. Soot belched from the tailpipes as shepherds soothed the goats, donkeys and two camels that rounded out their load.

"Where will I be riding?" Maggie saw the caravan stretched as far back as she could see.

"You can ride with us." Ashil opened the door and patted the seat. Ali looked over her head. "I think she's riding with Enver."

Maggie turned and saw Enver walking quickly toward her. He motioned to the lead truck. "You'll be riding with me."

"Why?" Maggie asked.

"Because I said so." Enver turned and headed toward the waiting truck, leaving her behind. Maggie ran to catch up. He got in and started the engine. She walked calmly to his side of the truck.

"Get in or get left behind, and I don't much care which one you choose," he said.

Maggie took a deep breath. "I'm not a child. Don't treat me like one." She walked around to the passenger side, climbed up into the cab and carefully closed the door.

"Why can't I ride with Ashil?" Enver's abruptness galled Maggie.

"The chief said I'm responsible for you. That means you ride with me," Enver said. "There are things you need to know before we make camp for the first night."

"Like what?" Maggie asked.

"Tonight, you won't have a sleeping room, or a toilet. You'll sleep under the truck in what you're wearing." Enver checked his mirror as trucks behind him maneuvered into a single file. He waved them forward with his left arm out the window. They lurched forward and Maggie heard chickens squawk in a chorus of protest.

☙

A sudden jolt caused Maggie to snork herself out of a deep sleep. She squinted at the sun. Would this day ever end? It couldn't possibly be as long as yesterday. Six words or maybe it was six sentences had been the sum of conversation from the moment they left the village until they camped for the night.

"You're snoring," Enver said. "And you're lying on my arm, sit up."

"Are we there yet?" Maggie groaned. She glanced out the rear window and saw the sea of goats and sheep, smelled them too. "I need a bath, about seven hours long, with lots of bubbles, scalding hot water, thick white towels, more hot water …"

"None of that where we're going. I do like a night in the hamam myself," Enver said.

"I'll bet you do," Maggie said.

"Hamam, not harem. Turkish bath. You're not awake." Enver navigated around a boulder.

"How much longer?" Maggie sniffed her underarm.

"Today, or total?" Enver asked.

"Both, and you know what I mean." She sighed and touched her dirty hair.

"Not much farther," Enver said.

"You said that this morning."

"Not as far as when we started."

"You sound like my mother," Maggie said.

"Tell me about your mother," Enver said.

"Not today." Maggie checked the lock then leaned against the cab door. She adjusted various camel-hair bags of food between them. She grimaced as they fell into a bone-jarring hole.

All she ever asked was to not die alone in a hospital with a tube in her nose and a cold-eyed nurse looking up her backside. She died in a hospital, with a tube in her nose, I'm guessing. Probably a cold-eyed nurse looking up her backside, too. I don't know, I wasn't there.

Enver muttered under his breath. Maggie watched him wrestle to keep the truck out of deep ruts. There were no longer any villages, or stone houses dotting the mountainside. The road became a trail as trees became thicker, and small patches of dark grass began to appear.

"If we were on camels, this would take two weeks, not three days," Enver said.

"I don't think I would have lasted two weeks." Maggie welcomed any conversation. "Why the change?"

"When I came home from Europe I decided trucks to get to the yayla didn't take away from our culture. I suggested this to the men and the chief. We spoke about it for some time, then, the chief told me to get one, and he'd see."

"Aha, a western invention that was acceptable," Maggie answered in English. She needed a language break.

Stone the Goat

"Yes, but one of a very few." Enver slipped easily into English, smiling.

"The women didn't get to suggest something, I take it?"

"Of course not. Never to be allowed," Enver said.

"You men are afraid. That must be it," Maggie replied.

A ghost of a smile danced across Enver's lip. "Absolutely not."

"Absolutely so," Maggie said, returning the smile.

After the next turn, a clearing appeared. Enver drove as far as he could into a grassy meadow. The caravan of vehicles exited the narrow road to form a loose circle.

Maggie pushed open the door with a grunt. She slid out of the truck and smelled moisture in the air. The ground here was softened by the water, and full of abundant grass in this hollow of the mountain's throat.

Enver unlatched the trailer gate and laid it down to form a ramp for the goats to exit in a tumble. He whistled and a young shepherd came running.

"Take them to that grazing spot." Enver pointed to a grove of scrubby trees. "There's a stream there, but don't let them drink north of the crossing."

The shepherd, staff in hand, scampered toward the trees with two dogs nudging errant sheep and goats toward the water.

Enver ran his hand through his hair. "Last night you joined Ashil and Ali for the evening meal. The chief told me to tell you that tonight you have to cook for me."

"You're kidding me," Maggie said.

"No, it's part of learning how to become a nomad woman. I'll start the fire for you, but I want to eat soon. There's a lot to do."

"I can start the fire," Maggie said.

"I said I'd do it." Enver wiped his face with his shirt tail.

"All the other women make the fires. If I am being tested on my skills as a nomad woman, I'll build my own." Maggie took the bundle of sticks and branches from behind the seat of the truck and scouted the area for the best place to make her small fire.

As the water boiled for tea, Maggie searched for the felt pad to lay the rug, or correctly, kilim and tablecloth on. Sometimes one's own language was a comfort in and of itself. Rug, flat weave rug. That's what a kilim was and would be called tonight. A plain rug. Where was it? She dug around in the woolen bags of food and sundries. She heard the hiss of the water boiling over into the fire, and sprang to move it. At last she found the felt, laid it on the ground, covered it in the clean rug and tablecloth and placed a large metal tray in the center. She filled it with goat jerky, boiled eggs, green almonds, salt, olives, yogurt, flat bread, honey and figs.

"I smelled the tea." Enver nodded appreciatively at the tray, laden with food.

"I'm supposed to tell the chief if you can cook, and he doesn't want more than one of us getting sick—"

"What?" Maggie felt a slow burn creeping up her spine.

"Join me. Let's get this done. I have to see the men before we leave tomorrow."

"Are you sure? Shouldn't I sit over there by myself?" Maggie asked.

"No, you should eat first. I'll watch you and if nothing happens I'll try some. Sit down and eat."

Maggie squatted to the ground. She jerked the şalvar around her legs and reached for a piece of flat bread. She might have to eat but she wouldn't sit. She filled the bread with goat jerky, peeled an egg and mashed it into the meat and bread. She topped it with olives and folded it into a Turkish tortilla. She ate quickly, made another, and then scooped honey into a third piece of bread. "I'm not dead yet so it must be okay to eat, huh?" Maggie said.

Enver reached for the bread, filled it and began eating. He was watching her. She didn't care.

"The jerky is good, did Ashil make it?" Enver helped himself.

"Yes," Maggie said. "I made the eggs, yogurt and flat bread."

"Enver slid a dried fig off the raffia rope and held it out to Maggie. She took the fig. She smelled the rich fragrance and rolled it around in her mouth.

"Where did you learn to make such a good fire?" Enver sipped his tea.

Maggie studied him carefully. How much information did she want to give to this man she couldn't trust? "I grew up in a lot of places. My father taught me how to make a fire."

"Wanderers, kind of like us?" He offered her another fig.

"Kind of," she accepted.

Enver slid a fig off the rope for himself. "And where is your father?"

"Don't know. He left us one day, said he would never be able to stay in one place. Never saw him again."

"Are you like him?" He leaned back against the truck and looked at Maggie.

Maggie caught her breath and looked at Enver's black and impenetrable eyes. She saw nothing that would make her share any part of her life with this man who really was a stranger. She reached for the jerky and slapped it into the bag. "None of your business." She poured the olives over the jerky and tied the top into a knot. And she had thought they could have a civil conversation. She could feel his eyes on her as she picked up the food and quickly folded up the cloth and felt. "If you're not sick you could just go now," she said.

Sparks from the small fire spewed upward into the dusky sky. Enver stood up and yawned. "I don't seem to be sick, but time will tell. I'm going to see the chief. Knit some of your socks with the women, you could use some help on that. I'll be back."

Maggie stuffed the tin dishes, food and felt pad into the bundles that would rest near her feet tomorrow. One more day and this trip would be over. Tonight, she would do exactly as she pleased. It would not include knitting or conversation with any women. She wanted some time alone, to think in English, to simply sit and watch the heavens. Yes, one more day and she'd be with Ashil and Ali. Ali never bothered her. She stood still a moment to collect herself. Maggie started laughing. Her life had come down to wishing, wanting to spend time with a nomad woman and milking goats!

As the dusk deepened, camels snorted and weaved their way to the ground. Children laughed in simple games and women gathered around small fires to gossip. Somewhere on the far side of the circle Maggie heard the faint sound of a flute.

She picked up a long stick to navigate around some of the stones and wandered a short distance from the fireside. Here, in the semi-darkness she could see the shadows, hear the sounds of laughter floating across the meadow.

A last streak of purple floated on the western horizon. In the east, the moon was full, a deep golden ball; each end of the earth competing against itself for the beauty prize.

Footsteps startled her. She turned to see who was encroaching on her spot.

Enver stopped just short of the rock she sat on. "What are you doing here?"

"Watching the stars," she said.

"I told you to join the women," Enver said.

"Yes, you did."

"You didn't do it."

"You're right, I didn't." Maggie said.

"Go back to the camp."

Maggie's voice hardened. "I'll go when I'm ready."

Enver stood a moment. "Move over."

"What?" she asked.

"Move over. I'm going to sit with you," Enver said.

"You can't. I'm a woman." Maggie didn't budge.

"You're not a Turkish woman. Everyone thinks you belong to me."

"You know better." Maggie spun sideways, eyes flashing.

"But of course." He pulled out a cigarette, rubbed it between his fingers, glanced at her and then tucked it back inside his pocket. He leaned against the rock.

The night was too beautiful to ignore. Maggie swept her hand across the great expanse of sky. "The stars are so bright here."

"These are the same stars you see in London, or Paris, except there you can hardly see them for all the city lights."

"Oh, stop it." Maggie looked at Enver. "I need this moment."

"So do I," Enver said. See that bright star directly above you?"

Another shower of sparks from the fire illuminated Enver's eyes. He cupped her face in one hand, his thumb on her cheekbone, waiting, pulled her to him, daring her to move, to protest before his mouth bore down on hers with the fury of a warrior thundering down the Anatolian plains.

Shocked by a surge of desire, Maggie responded with a fierceness she could not comprehend, stuck her nose into his neck and beard, sucked his smell into her—soap, smoke, something farther back in time—stallions and sultans; drank his taste into her mouth—figs, raki, tobacco, man—that was it, man, until she gasped for air. She opened her eyes and jerked away from Enver. She glimpsed the turbaned chief before she lost her balance and dropped backward off the rock.

Stone the Goat

A searing pain filled her head before she faded into welcome nothingness.

☙

She heard voices chattering, Enver and Ashil's, something about her being in a faint for some time. A blinding light flooded Maggie's eye. She struggled to sit up.

"Be still. I think you have a concussion." Enver snapped off the flashlight and stuck it in his pocket.

"What happened?" Maggie touched her head tenderly.

"You fell backward off that rock and hit your head. I couldn't catch you."

Maggie tried to roll the other way and sit up, but a wave of nausea kept her flat.

"Don't sit up. You've been out for a few minutes. Ashil is here to help you, and then I'll see that you stay awake tonight." Enver ignored her waving hand. "There's nothing to discuss."

Maggie could hear Ashil's quick feet. She heard the tinkle of a spoon in a tea glass and Ashil's quiet tut-tutting.

"Here, drink this." Ashil held Maggie's head up for a tiny swallow. "You'll be better soon. I'll wash your face."

"Ashil, really, you don't have to do this," Maggie mumbled.

"Yes, I must. The women want to know if you kiss men in America."

"Not in a long time." Maggie closed her eyes but the chief's face kept staring back at her. "But I just did a stupid thing." Maggie sucked in her breath when she turned her head. How stupid it was remained to be seen.

"The women want to know," Ashil laughed a little nervously, "they want to know if you want to marry Enver. We think he doesn't want to marry. He brought a woman with light hair and skin to the village and she stayed only a little while." She leaned over and lowered her voice. "If Enver doesn't want you now Tamay says you can have her husband for free. He can have a second wife because she never had a child. I think she's just mad at him, though." She stared into Maggie's eyes. "I've never had a child, either," she paused. "You don't want Ali, do you?"

"No." Maggie held her hand to her head and shook it gently. "No, I just want—"

"Good." Ashil breathed a sigh of relief. "I see Enver, so I'll go and come to you in the morning." Ashil rose to leave.

Maggie reached out and touched Ashil's hand. "Tell Enver that if he comes to sit with me all I want is a bottle of raki, and a clean glass."

Ashil nodded and walked quickly in the direction of the still glowing fires sprinkled around the meadow. Maggie could see her in conversation with Enver. They both glanced her way, then Enver stalked toward the chieftain's truck and Ashil scurried straight toward Ali.

☙

"My head hurts." Maggie touched the sizeable knot on the side of her head. Her left eye, newly bruised, and its companion, an elongated blue-black streak down her jaw line rounded out the triad of Maggie's discomfort. She bounced hard in the seat of the truck. "Ouch." The memory of a kiss and a big glass of raki flooded her as she ran a thick tongue over bruised lips.

"You drank too much raki last night." Enver shifted the growling gears.

"That has nothing to do with this," Maggie mumbled through the pain.

"It certainly does. I was amazed at how much you consumed." He winced. "You look terrible."

"I fell off a rock. You thought I had a concussion." She shifted in the seat to face him. "And the chief being there the very moment you took advantage of me? Did you set me up?"

"I didn't know he was there," Enver said.

"Which doesn't help me, does it?" Maggie yelped. "Why did you kiss me? I just wanted to be alone for one minute. I'll be the one that pays."

"Look, I didn't plan it, I didn't know he was there but I am quite sure I didn't take advantage of you." Enver shifted gears in controlled savagery.

Maggie switched to petty. "You had a flashlight; that I *can* remember."

"Yes, I did. So?" Enver said.

"Wow. A western invention you find useful," Maggie dove into cattiness.

Enver ignored her remark. "You had a knot on your head that swelled, but the rest ... You don't remember, do you?" He shook his head. "You insisted on dancing around Reza and fell over my saddle."

"The shepherd?" Maggie asked.

"That Reza. He was sitting on it, quieting the sheep with his flute until you decided to dance." Enver shot her a glance. "You hit your eye and chin. Remember now?"

"No." Maggie looked out the truck window. She didn't want to remember much about the previous night. "Why do you carry that saddle anyway? It's for a camel. You're driving a truck."

"I'll use it in the yayla. My grandfather used it to tame camels in the days when we owned the desert. When he died, my father didn't want it and gave it to me."

You love the smelly thing. Just like Robert and that battered old lunchbox.

Maggie stuffed a small bag of wool under her head, and turned to the window. Every muscle she had screamed for attention. The dull throbbing headache took second place to the not-so-dull pain in her shoulder. Had she really danced around in a drunken state? Did the chief see that? Why didn't Enver just shut her up in the truck, for God's sake? "Did the chief see me last night?" Maggie mumbled the question.

"Do you mean," Enver enunciated carefully, "when you were drinking and dancing?"

"Yeah, that when," Maggie knew the answer.

"No. Ali took him to the rear of the trucks, and the men had their raki and smoking there. "Enver turned his head and looked directly at Maggie. "Ali did that for Ashil. Thank her."

Maggie rode silently. If she hadn't responded to Enver's kiss it would have been over and maybe the chief wouldn't have been there at the wrong moment to see it. On the other hand, maybe he would have. It was what it was and only she would have to deal with the fallout.

Hours later, after a lunch in the truck of dried meat and bread, and an afternoon of smoother ruts and more stands of trees, more streams and sweeter air, a sudden turn off the road and the truck rumbled to its final stop.

Enver creaked open the door and lifted his face into a gentle breeze. His three-day old beard was speckled black and white against his brown skin. His black hair was swept back under a brown turban. His white cotton shirt, cuffs turned up twice, loose cotton trousers the shade of desert sand and scuffed work boots were covered in black dust. Soot from the diesel engine filled the fine lines around his tired eyes, and clung in a half moon to the bronze skin of his upper lip.

Maggie opened her door and the breeze caressed them both.

Lush undulating grass and gentle green hills stretched to the mountains peaks, and groves of trees stood like ramrod soldiers nearby.

Enver turned to Maggie with a weary sigh. "We're here. You have survived the long trip to the upper yayla."

A pang of regret nicked Maggie's conscience. She had accused him of a set up with the chief. Now she wasn't so sure. She wasn't sure of anything except that if she didn't get to wash soon she might die.

"I've survived. Thank you." The other trucks rolled past,

no longer in need of a leader. They stopped at varying intervals, disgorging women who carried sacks and bundles, wood for fires, and buckets for water. Children tumbled from the trucks and shrieked with delight at their freedom.

Maggie unloaded the bags of food, bundle of wood and her duffle bags. Ashil approached, slightly out of breath. Together they gazed in wonder as hundreds of goats, sheep, dogs, and camels bleated, bounded, barked, snorted, and shepherds whistled, cajoled and shouted their way through the melee into a miraculous semblance of order.

"Welcome to the yayla," Ashil pointed her hand in a wide sweep to the backdrop of mountains, cloudless evening sky and verdant grass. "Our sheep will get so fat." She clapped her hands. "It's good to be home."

Chapter Nine

Someone beat a drum, a flute joined in and the song of a pent-up beast crackled through the tribe.

"Come, come. You no longer have to be with Enver." Ashil pulled Maggie toward a large tent being erected by seven tribesmen. "Here is where we'll live. Do you like it?"

"I do." All of Maggie's tiredness melted away in the shine of Ashil's eyes.

Soon tents dotted the landscape. The evening meals ended early and quietly. The tribe readied itself for the night. When darkness came, the Urek tribe went to sleep in the light of the full moon.

Maggie slept soundly and without dreams that first night. She woke early and slipped out her tent flap to see the beginnings of a yayla morning.

Free of their saddles, donkeys nosed the grass in contentment. Maggie lifted her head to catch the smell of wood smoke. The tribe was waking up.

Her eyes followed a trail of sheep coursing its way up a small rise to a day of grazing. Tall grass slapped at the feet of a shepherd whose donkey moved slowly at the end of the flock. Two dogs bounded ahead, a faint bark warning a stray to return to the fold.

Maggie heard footsteps and saw Enver from the corner of her eye. "What's that?" She pointed to a caravan of trucks on a far hillside.

"Another tribe." The jubilation in Enver's voice couldn't be contained. "We'll be together in a few days. It's time."

At his feet several ewes nuzzled his leg, hungry and impatient for their trek to the grazing ground.

"I'm going with the sheep today. I've been gone too long from my job."

Maggie saw the black wool fez on his clean hair, the old sandy colored shirt, and coarse wool trousers captured at his waist with a belt of eagle motifs, the sign of the Urek tribe. He smelled of almond soap.

"Who are you?" Maggie stood between him and a gray donkey. "Haluk told me you lived eight years in London, went to school and loved a good suit. Then you bring me here and become this shepherd, this goat herder ... I don't know what."

"I have a degree from Manchester University and a second one from London School of Economics," Enver said.

"You're a graduate of London School of Economics?" Maggie asked slowly.

"Yes," Enver said.

Maggie studied the ground in front of her for a long moment. "You went to school with some of the smartest women in the world, and you believe," she pointed to a group of women on their way to milk, "they shouldn't have a say over their lives?"

"I'll talk to you about this tonight." Enver straddled the stout donkey and called the dogs.

"And you'll answer that question," Maggie said.

In moments the herd was trotting past her and the tent on the path to the meadows. He led them up the rise where they joined another flock and melded into an ocean of sheep that slowly disappeared in the undulating hills.

Maggie turned slowly to take in the scene before her. She was here. The upper yayla. She said it several times. Upper yayla. Here with the Urek nomad tribe, just like she promised Mr. Beyter. She had milked and churned and worked wool and knitted, (sort of), survived the giant ram injuries, exposed herself to Enver and Ashil and kissed the first man since Robert. That last little thing gave the chief ammunition to use against her if he chose. Nothing had come of that, yet.

Maggie breathed deeply in the clear air. On the other hand, she had made a friend in Ashil, been accepted by the other women as an apprentice nomad and met an old woman as wise as her mother.

In these first weeks she had re-learned to live as she had in the past. No one knew, except Mr. Beyter, Robert, and a few others that she had grown up living in places without indoor plumbing, moved every few months to follow the construction worker trade of her father, and after he had left, joined her mother and the migrant farm workers who swarmed the South. She had worked just as hard harvesting crops as these women did working the wool. Maybe that was what drew her here. Maybe that was what Mr. Beyter had counted on.

Maggie caught a wafting scent of bread on the air. She followed her nose to the back side of a large black tent near a bend in the gurgling stream of water that ran along the grove of trees. Against an earthen embankment rocks had been placed to protect a fire from three sides.

There, in the early morning cool Hala tended the fire and made fresh bread. She sat cross-legged, rhythmically rolling the smooth rod over the dough, placed on a small scarred table. She placed each piece, one by one on the metal dome over the fire, and then stacked them on a tray nearby.

"Morning." Maggie squatted beside Hala. "Are you happy to be in the yayla?"

Hala sucked in a breath of the cool air and closed her eyes. "This is my home. I'm happy."

"I haven't had a chance to talk to you since we left the village." Maggie shoved some limbs into the fire.

"No." Hala sat back and eyed Maggie. "The chief says you're a loose woman and that we're to stay away from you." She sucked a twig between her teeth and studied Maggie carefully.

Maggie sat down hard on the ground, and wrapped her arms around her stomach. "I made a mistake. I shouldn't have kissed Enver. He kissed me first and I shouldn't have had any raki. This isn't all my fault—well, the raki is."

Hala lifted another piece of flat bread from the metal sheet. "I knew a loose woman, once, in our village in the north."

Maggie sat mutely. She should have stayed in the village,

gone back to Antalya with Haluk, never kissed Enver and never ever come to this damn country …

Hala looked at Maggie intently. "You, I think, are not one."

Maggie swallowed hard, and scooted closer to Hala. She turned her face to the mountains, and bit her cheek to collect herself. She leaned over and wiped her face with her sleeve. "Thank you."

Hala too, gazed at the mountains. After a long silence she reached over and patted Maggie's arm. "It's not so hard you know. Old women like me, we can smell the truth." She handed Maggie a hot piece of bread and stared at her with black bean eyes. "Keep your smell."

༄

It was mid-evening when Enver returned. The sheep had been milked high in the pasture. Copper cans of milk bounced along the sides of the five donkeys in his entourage. He dismounted and handed the animals off to a gaggle of apprentice shepherds.

He stretched high, turned his neck slowly and caught sight of Maggie feeding the chickens. He stood, waiting. "Come here. We can talk now." He lit a cigarette and the tip glowed faintly red.

"No. You should rest. Perhaps have a glass of tea." Maggie tossed the last handful of crumbs to the hens. "Join me later." She lifted the flap and disappeared into her corner of the tent. Let him wait on her for a while.

Enver returned much sooner than she expected and called

for her at her small door flap. She stepped out to join him. The fez was gone. His black hair caught the glint of the evening sun. He leaned against the rock outcropping, lit a cigarette and blew a lazy smoke ring into the air.

"So, you had questions for me. I'm ready," he said.

Maggie dove in. "Who are you?"

"My mother was from this tribe."

"So was Mr. Beyter' mother," Maggie said.

"Yes. That's true." Enver blew another smoke ring.

"And what about your father?" Maggie pressed on.

"He met my mother in a market near Manavgat. She was selling prayer rugs and water bags for the camels."

"Was he a nomad too?" Maggie's interest piqued.

"No, he was a farmer who came to market. His parents spoke to her parents, told them that their son was interested, my mother knitted him a courting sock, which he accepted." Enver ground the butt of the cigarette out with his heel.

"What happened?" Maggie leaned forward.

"He married her, took her to Silifke, she got sick during childbirth, died and he brought me back here to the tribe. I grew up with my grandparents," he folded his arms, "then they died and Hala and the old chief gave me a life in the yayla every summer." His face softened. "It was good then."

"And in the winter?" Maggie asked.

"My father made me attend school in Antalya," Enver said.

Maggie sat quietly on the rock. Two different worlds. She knew what that was like. She had sat in classrooms with well-clad children, aching to be one of them, knowing her world on the grinding side of poverty was a chasm she couldn't cross. "Was it hard for you to go back and forth?"

"I hated it." Enver stared at the mountains. "I didn't belong at the school … no one else rode camels and ate yufka, and when I came back here, I was always the outsider."

"And how do you know Haluk?" Maggie asked.

"He's my brother." Enver's surprise was genuine. "That's why I volunteered to bring you here."

"Brother?" Maggie's heart raced. "I didn't know that."

"Half-brother. When my mother died, my father left me here and went to the city. He married again and Haluk is ten years younger than me."

"But, your names are different." Maggie listened as if from the bottom of a well.

"I kept the name of my mother and this tribe."

A pounding erupted in Maggie's head. She couldn't hear what Enver was saying. All this time Maggie had thought she was making her own way. The chief was right. She *was* being handed off from man to man whether she liked it or not. Damn them all.

Maggie slid off the rock. "I have to go." She flew through the flap into her little room. She heard Enver's low voice through the carpet walls.

"I didn't know Haluk hadn't told you," he said.

☙

Sleep eluded her, and a mantle of self-pity slowly enveloped her in a gray shroud. Maggie could have been in Antalya, or

London, or Cairo or anywhere else in the world she wanted to be; doing projects for the Beyter Charitable Foundation. She could be lolling on the beach in Limasol, Cyprus, or poking around bazaars in Algiers with Lahli.

Haluk had lied to her, never telling her or even hinting at who Enver was. And Enver, he hadn't respected or defended her to the chief. He still believed if she hadn't disobeyed Ashil the breeding ram wouldn't have been stoned for no good reason. In the blackness of her little room she took her quilt and snugged it tightly around her. She buried her head in her small pillow to muffle the torrent of hot tears. Robert hadn't lied to her. He had respected her. And she had put off the one thing that he had ever truly asked of her.

Memories of the annual Meadows family reunion sprang unbidden into her mind. It had been a huge affair. When they had first married, Robert had warned Maggie of the one week he would never give up. It was his family's get-together at the ancestral ranch, complete with bunkhouses, horses, cattle, home cooking, hand turned ice cream, giant watermelons, fishing and swimming. It was a time for Robert's two sisters and three brothers, complete with their broods, to shriek, and laugh at old family photos, to re-tell stories for the umpteenth time, and fall exhausted over one another at the end of the day for a to-the-death game of Scrabble.

Robert was doubtless the favorite uncle, in part because he rarely missed a baseball game or dance recital. His favorite family photo had been one with all eleven of his nieces and nephews, from toddler to teen-ager, sitting on top of, next to and wrapped around him on the front porch swing.

Promises. Maggie had promised her mother she wouldn't die alone, and she had broken it. She had promised Robert a child, broken that one too. He had patiently waited for her, but no, she had put herself first, her wants and desires; put her career and wanderlust ahead of everything, including him. Five years she had said, let me have five years, but he didn't have that long. Now, she could be holding a part of him, a child who would have had his smile, his laugh, perhaps a boy who would have inherited that ridiculous, stupid, ugly, black, beautiful, treasured family heirloom lunchbox.

☙

"You're late today from your room." Ashil handed Maggie a glass of steaming tea. "Are you sick?"

"No." Maggie studied the tea glass intently. Her eyes were swollen, and red, she was sure.

"Enver came by this morning." Ashil poured herself a glass. "What did he want?"

"To see if we had taken in a lamb to watch." She added sugar and stirred it slowly. "He said he heard moaning, like a lamb, or a sick ewe." She eyed Maggie closely. "I told him we didn't have a lamb. Was it you?"

Maggie smiled wanly. "I must have had a bad dream." She drank the tea. "I'll be fine."

Maggie was ignored as the tribe fell into an orchestrated harmony of constructing their summer homes. The men busied themselves cleaning out the pine branches and limbs that had piled up in the corrals and around the huts. They saved the sturdy ones; put them in piles to use for other tents and shelters. Children broke up the smaller branches into pieces to use for cooking, and stacked the brushy limbs away to use to mend the corrals.

There was no waste here, Maggie thought as she helped two young girls carry a load of firewood to Hala's tent. The grouping of tents, twenty or so, were closer together than the homes in the village.

Enver spoke from over Maggie's shoulder. He stopped next to her, his arms full of large pieces of pine wood. "It's not the village, is it?"

"No, it isn't, but I think this is who you really are." She gazed around at the kaleidoscope of color, deep shades of red, green, blue, brilliant white and cream and yellow, dark brown, black, orange, and pink that hung as walls from every tent she could see.

Maggie had realized that Enver was at a loss as to why Haluk hadn't told her of their relationship. She couldn't hold that against him. She did, however, have a few questions for Haluk, and it might be best that she wouldn't see him until the end of this trip.

"You didn't see these carpets in the village, did you?" Enver spoke over the armful of wood.

"No, I saw the ones in the looms, and they certainly weren't like these." Maggie wanted to go and rub her face against each one.

"This is the life we can't afford to lose." He shifted the

wood and walked toward a large wood pile. "This is who we've always been."

Maggie completed a sweep of the encampment, and headed back to Ashil's tent. She had spent a month adjusting to life in the village. She had managed to get this far, and now, the real test would begin.

∽

It had taken two days of hard work but the camp was set up, and life in the crisp air and vastness of the upper yayla had begun.

"What are we doing today?" Maggie arrived back at the tent from milking. She brushed pine needles off the hem of her şalvar.

Ashil wiped her hands on her apron. "Today is special. We're going to Hala's to see what we can do to help Sema and Leslihan."

Maggie listened for a moment. "Why is it so silent?"

"The men and boys have all gone to visit with the Saz tribe. Over there." She pointed to a distant grouping of tents. "Today, we are without our husbands, fathers and sons. Come, come." Ashil stopped Maggie before they arrived at Hala's. "I need to tell you something. You have to sit at the edge of the group. No one is going to speak to you until we hear that you aren't a loose woman."

Maggie sighed and accepted the weight of embarrassment. She had believed her explanation to Hala had been sufficient. She thought back since their arrival. All the tribe had been busy, and she had been ignored. Not from their busyness apparently.

Hala's tent was an anthill of women and toddlers who had gathered early. Young girls sat next to their mothers, babies nursed or rested on the laps of friends as mothers drank tea. Young teens sat together comparing embroidery work. The group ignored Maggie and looked to Hala for direction. Hala, with her wispy hair sticking out from her scarf, sat on a folded carpet near the back of the tent. Hala surveyed the women before her carefully. She made eye contact with them all, and then rested her eyes on Maggie.

Hala waved Maggie to a seat next to her. "Come," she pointed to a spot to the left of her, "sit with me today." With that simple gesture the label 'loose woman' was brushed aside like old goat droppings and the women once again smiled at Maggie. Hala pointed to a spot to the right of her seat. "Ashil, sit here."

Hala shifted around to find Sema. "You have a wedding, and what do you want us to do for Leslihan?"

"Her wedding carpet is finished. We want to show it to you before her mother-in-law-to-be comes to see it," Sema said.

A young mother nodded to Sema. "Oh, she'll say the weave is too tight or too loose, or the colors are not of her tribe."

"What are they talking about?" Maggie whispered to Ashil.

"The groom's mother and her family will come to inspect Leslihan's handiwork. If it isn't good, she won't allow her son to marry Leslihan." Ashil whispered back as the other women chattered about memories of their own wedding carpets.

Stone the Goat

Hala cast a disapproving glance at Maggie and Ashil. She adjusted herself on the carpets and harrumphed for attention.

"Maggie doesn't know our marriage customs. I will tell her some things, and all of you," she waved her hand lazily around the group, "will tell her the things that I forget because I am old." She closed her eyes, and the women fell silent watching her.

"Our daughters leave us, just as I left my family and my home near the Black Sea. I was born in the season of the new lambs, they tell me, some seventy-five years ago. In my sixteenth year, I saw a young boy in the yayla. He was a good shepherd; he found the best grass for the goats and his eyes ... they were very kind."

A young girl bounced up and down with glee. "And you knitted a perfect sock to catch him!"

"It's true." Hala opened one eye and smiled at the girl. "I was the best knitter in our tribe. We had no villages then." She sighed faintly. "We roamed the whole of Anatolia, and knew all the tribes from the sea to the north to the sea to the south." She lingered a moment in that pocket of her memory. "Where was I? Yes, my father and mother took the sock to his parents, and told them that they wished to offer me to their son to be his wife."

"Did anyone ask the boy?" Maggie couldn't wait.

Hala took a sip of her tea, twirled wool on her spindle and closed her eyes again. "Ah, you are too quick with the questions. The boy's parents asked what dowry I came with, and my father said two silk carpets, four wool ones, two camels, twelve sheep, six goats and one donkey."

"A very good dowry," Ashil spoke boldly. A consenting murmur rounded the room.

"Yes, a good dowry, but the boy's mother insisted, as is her right, to come and see my carpets, kilims and my camel saddle coverings. She wanted to taste my cooking and see my wool dyeing technique," Hala said.

Maggie spoke in a low voice, "Because you became her property."

"It's true. We all left our homes to move to our husband's family. We worked for our husband's mother. If she was a generous woman, it could be a good life; if she chose to not speak to us, we might work for years without much happiness."

"And what kind was she?" Maggie forgot there were other women in the room. She needed to know.

"She liked my work and agreed with my parents that it would be a good match. She said if her son returned the sock within three days, he wanted to marry me."

"Did he?" Maggie pressed.

"He did. I married my shepherd and became a good daughter-in-law to his mother."

Maggie released her breath. "That's good news to hear."

"It was only for three seasons. She died of a winter cough the year my son was born."

"I didn't know you had a son," Maggie said.

Hala sat a long moment. "He died before he was out of the cradle."

Maggie knew then that Hala's compassion for her sprang

from the deep well of a wounded soul.

One of the nursing mothers handed Hala a small child, wrapped in a soft pink blanket. Hala took the infant, bent her head low and rocked gently. Maggie stifled her tears at the sight of the tiny bundle cradled in the splotchy arms of the old Madonna.

Chapter Ten

MAGGIE PUSHED HER scarf backward, hunched over the stream bed and scooped water into a copper pitcher. She squinted at the cloudless sky and wiped perspiration from her neck. Summer was coming.

The previous day Leslihan's groom, his mother and her entourage had arrived at the camp. They were from the Urgaz tribe that grazed in another part of the vast yayla. All of the women hoped Leslihan's handwork and dowry of household goods would please the visiting mother-in-law. Maggie stayed on the periphery to catch a glimpse of the young groom-to-be. Ashil pinched Maggie when the groom came into view.

"Very handsome," Maggie whispered.

Ashil nodded in agreement. "I think so too. Leslihan will have beautiful children."

But that was yesterday. Today was a water-toting day. Maggie fitted a clay stopper into the neck and then filled two buckets nearly to the brim. With a halter made of rope, she positioned the pitcher on her back and picked up the buckets.

Maggie's back ached from the endless trips to the stream. Her left arm, neck and both shoulders throbbed in a constant dull pain. She glanced at the blood that trickled from a deep scrape on her knuckles. The compression sleeve had to be doing its work, because the swelling was kept to a minimum. She pushed up the long sleeve of her blouse to adjust the brown elastic sleeve. Every day she worked at something that exacerbated the problem.

A young girl with a basket filled with plants jumped out of a thicket of flowers. The child ran to Maggie and pirouetted in the path.

"Hello there." Maggie set the buckets down. "What's in your basket?"

"Dyers Woad, Madder Red and Ox-eye." The child held it out for Maggie to see the pile of green plants, brown roots and yellow flowers. "Tomorrow we dye the wool."

"I know." Maggie pointed to the buckets. "I'm filling up the pots. It takes a lot of water, doesn't it?"

"Yes." The small girl giggled and skipped along in front of Maggie, stopping to pick more of the large yellow flowers that bunched in profusion along the path. "It takes a lot of flowers, too."

Maggie trudged on toward her goal. She hefted the buckets and carefully poured the water into the first of the black pots situated at the far end of the village. She slid the heavy pitcher from her back and sank down on the ground. She heard footsteps and saw the chief stop near her knees.

"Don't get comfortable. You're not finished with your work today." He leaned against a pot.

"I'm not comfortable. I'm resting a minute." Maggie didn't lift her eyes or move. "I know my job and I'm doing it."

Stone the Goat

The chief moved closer. Maggie could smell his shoes. She saw the dirt on his socks. *If you were Ashil's husband she would scrub your socks until they were as white as a hotel sheet and then she'd scrub you.*

"You're not invited to stand so close to me." Maggie made no move to get up.

The chief didn't move. "Honorable women don't leave their husbands."

"I didn't leave my husband. He died."

"What did Mustafa Beyter see in you?" The chief asked.

Maggie stood up and stepped into the cloud of foul breath that separated them. She stood on her toes, thrust her chin toward him. "Look at me."

The chief blinked.

Maggie moved closer. "He saw a smart woman, like Lahli, in me. You know, *your* Lahli, from this very tribe, the *woman* who keeps your sheep safe so you can have the best herds and get the best prices."

The chief turned his head away from her in disgust. "Where are your brothers, or uncles? They would tell you your place and know how to and control you."

"I told you I don't have any brothers." Very carefully Maggie picked up the buckets and the pitcher. Speaking slowly and enunciating each word in perfect Turkish she said, "I do have good ears and I know what you've been saying about me. I am not a loose woman or any of the other names you've called me."

"You are a disgrace to Allah and to women who know their

place," he said. The loathing in his voice was thick, "But you'll learn. And you'll pay for such disrespect to me."

"And you are a donkey's ass", Maggie said storming past him, empty buckets banging at her knees, the pitcher thudding against her hip.

"I heard you," the chief said to her fast moving back.

Maggie stood at the stream. She lifted the copper pitcher with a grunt, slipped the harness over her shoulders, and hefted it to the tops of her hips. She balanced the load with a bucket of water in each hand. She would pay. Somehow, he would make her pay. She had insulted him beyond his duty to Mr. Beyter's goodwill. She had given the chief cause, again, to send her back, and this time there had been no witnesses. It was possible to disappear in these mountains and no one would ever know what happened to her.

She moved with dread up the path and into a welcome shade of a thick grove of trees. She could see the corral just ahead, and the big breeding ram feeding there, alone. He was still used to sire lambs, but he no longer reigned supreme in the herd. She heard rapid footsteps behind her.

A sickening thud between her shoulder blades and a searing pain sheared the breath out of her. She stumbled. A second thud in the same place—she fell to her knees and over the buckets. She gasped for air, any air, any tiny bit of it at all to fill the vast void in her lungs. Finally, she caught her breath and opened her eyes.

She lay in the puddle of water, still gurgling from the pitcher on her back. The pain in her back pulsed its way to the farthest nerves in her body. She slid out of the halter and crawled to her knees, searching for whatever had stunned her so completely. Spasms of pain flooded her body. She crawled around on the path and finally found them. A smooth stone, the size of her two fists, rested in the trampled grass of the path. Near it lay a second one, larger and not so smooth.

Maggie hunched in a tight ball, her clothes soaking up the water. There was very little of her back exposed when she had the harness on. Someone had accurate aim.

It hadn't taken him long. Slowly she heaved herself up. Haluk had told her not to come, more than once. Enver didn't think she would last and hadn't changed his mind. There were inviolate rules that one never crossed in this culture. Defying a tribal chief ranked high on the list.

Who could she tell? Except for gigantic bruises she knew were in the making, she could prove nothing. Who would believe her?

In the meantime, the water for the dyeing pots couldn't wait. Slowly, Maggie stood up. The pain in her back had diffused from screaming sharp to teeth clenching sharp. Maggie picked up the stones and dropped one into each pocket. They would not be used as weapons against anyone else.

Maggie trudged back along the path to the spring, placed the two rocks behind a boulder and started all over again. The blister rising on her heel was a testament to her doggedness. She cursed herself with every step. Mr. Beyter had been a prisoner of war, had really suffered, and all she had was a toady chief to deal with. She should shut up and stop antagonizing him. He was goading her. Mr. Beyter had learned the art of self-control and patience. Her mother would have said that the only way out is through, and handled him with steely grace and aplomb. Why couldn't she?

Much later Maggie poured the last of the water into the pot and collected the empty buckets and water jar to take to Ashil's. On the eighteenth and final trip she picked up the stones from behind the boulder and put one into each pocket of her şalvar.

Hala walked by and inspected the pots and the fire wood beneath them. "It's good. The pots are full." Hala stuck her finger into the water and swished it around. "Tomorrow we dye our wool." She lifted her finger and let the water run down her hand. "You'll see how we make the colors of our tribe."

Maggie's thoughts were elsewhere. Would the chief do something else to her? She looked around carefully before heading back to Ashil's tent.

She heard the ram snorting when she passed the corral. He sensed her presence and turned his head and one good eye in her direction. Maggie hesitated, then walked over and rested her arms on the gate.

She stared at his thick white wool, the golden hair that covered his hooves, the horns that could have killed her. She had been a stranger, had entered his world and stoned him, put his eye out when he tried to do nothing more than defend his ewes and his rightful place as the prize ram.

Maggie leaned on the gate. "I had no right to go into your

Stone the Goat

pen before the other women got there." She didn't care who heard her. "You stood up for yourself and I stoned you. You were doing exactly what you should have done, protecting your ewes. The ram snorted once more and walked slowly toward her. He stopped just short of the fence and cocked his head, as if listening.

"Today I stood up for myself. The chief stoned me," she reached into her left pocket and pulled out the smooth stone. She reached into her right pocket and pulled out the larger, jagged one, "with these." Maggie held out the stones for the ram to see. She laid them on the ground just outside the corral gate, stood up and looked at him with grudging respect. "We're even."

Chapter Eleven

A SEMI-CIRCLE OF women gathered around Hala in the morning air. The old woman puttered around the steaming pots, mumbling, shushing children and shooing chickens out of her path. She studied the baskets of fresh plants, flowers and tree bark, all drying in the hot sun. Nearby, she had jars, baskets of dried flowers and plants, and wool sacks of roots and tree bark.

Maggie had thrashed about the night before. With no one to help her decide what to do, she thought of Mr. Beyter. He would have told her to keep her goal in mind, put the episode behind her and soldier on. It had worked for him. Her mother would have said be strong and focus on the finish line.

Hala pulled out various roots from a small brown sack. "From these we will make the dye for our carpets. This one," she pointed to a gnarled mass, "is madder root. It makes that deep red color in this pot."

Maggie stepped closer. The old masters of the Renaissance had used it as a standard color in their palettes. "And in here?" Maggie peered into a second pot.

"Dyers Woad. That's a plant that makes this dark blue." Hala's pleasure in the deep indigo color that bubbled contentedly before her was evident. "The best plants come from near the sea. Enver takes a truck and some of the men to get it."

"Enver had a lot of plants and roots in his truck when he brought me here," Maggie said.

"The indigo from the plains where there is no rain is dull." Ashil took the stick from Hala and stirred the blue water herself. "They're easier to get, but our tribe doesn't want them."

"I noticed that rich blue," Maggie pointed to the walls of the tents behind them, "and that dark red hanging everywhere. I wondered how you got such colors, and now I know."

Hala took the stick back from Ashil and stirred the water gently. "There are twenty different colors in an onion skin." There was a hint of boastfulness in her voice. "We can make them all. We learn from our mothers and our mother's mothers which colors to put together to make," she looked down at a kilim a child was playing on, "that pink, and that green."

She stood back and clasped her hands together in deep satisfaction. "This madder root red gives us the color, but if we don't add salt, or ash or wood bark or this," she held up a bag of iron shavings, "the color will bleed away."

"That's called a mordant," Maggie said. She knew that iron made a deep red, alum made a lighter shade and both were the additives that kept the color from fading.

"Ashil is the best dyer and one day she'll take my place," Hala said.

Maggie sighed, taking a turn at stirring the indigo pot. These women knew all the secondary and tertiary colors to combine with primary ones. A look at any of the pile carpets and kilims they wove for themselves showcased the wide palette of colors.

"The two of you should be instructors at a university," Maggie said.

Ashil lifted a ladle full of red water and poured it carefully back into the pot. "And this means what to us?"

"It means you're some of the smartest women I have ever met," Maggie said.

Hala grunted. "Watch that fire. It's your job today."

"Where are the men?" Maggie stoked the fire to keep the pot boiling. "I haven't seen them today."

"They're with the other tribes. They talk of sheep and crops and drink tea and raki; and leave us to make our weavings and do our woman things," Hala smiled at Maggie, "It's good, for them and us."

Her smile encouraged Maggie. "How is it good for you?"

"When we're down in the villages, all the men talk of who is the strongest one, who has the best ram, who has the biggest camel, who is the …"

"Biggest ass?" Maggie clapped her hand over her mouth.

"It's true on some days," Ashil laughed. "We want to tie them to camels and send them to the desert, but the camels come back home and so do the husbands. What can you do?"

☙

Maggie sat with Ashil at the front of their tent and viewed with suspicion the ugly skein of wool and the new knitting needles in a pile before her. A cool breeze blew the shirts on the clothesline. She had been mesmerized by the entire dyeing process. It was art and skill. The women created the colors of the tribe, all from a bunch of roots, plants, flowers and tree bark. And they did it along with everything else. Maggie marveled at their work and told them so.

But the knitting needles did not bode well for her. "When am I going to learn to read your carpets?"

"Hala will decide. Here, take this." Ashil handed Maggie the needles and wool, and picked up an embroidery hook for herself. "She thinks you're not trying enough with the knitting, and I thought some different needles might help you." She concentrated on embroidering the silky fabric in her lap. "I'm almost finished with this pillow cover."

Maggie held up her wool. "This is so ugly."

"Yes, but you have to work with it until you knit a perfect sock. That's the tradition."

"Of course," Maggie saw a small donkey clop by. The man riding it ignored them both. "He's been here four times." Maggie eyed the blanket under his saddle. It was a dull uneven brown, complimented by a yellow stripe of similar dullness.

"He wants to buy one of Ali's camels."

Maggie dropped all pretense of knitting. "How long does it take?" The man slid off the donkey and greeted the tribesmen gathered around the camel in question. With a practiced hand he carefully ran his fingers down her neck, feeling her chest and flanks, checking her teeth.

Ashil glanced up from the tiny embroidery stitches, "Oh,

a long time. It might take from one full moon to the next to come to a fair price. After he came the first time, Ali discussed it with the chief, then last week, all that talk with Enver and the other men when they sat outside the chief's tent? It was about the sale of this camel."

Maggie pondered the machinations surrounding the knobby-kneed droopy-eyed dromedary.

"I hope they come to an agreement soon," Maggie said. "We'll have to give that man his own tent."

Ashil bit a thread off with her teeth. "Ali wants to see how selling his camel might affect the rest of the tribe. Not so long ago we came here on camels. Ali and I had twelve or so back then." She sighed. "It's so much easier now, with the big trucks, and thanks to Enver we can make them go, but what if no truck engine would start? Then what?"

"You'd need a camel to go get the parts to start it, I guess. I hadn't thought about that." Maggie's perspective changed.

"Exactly." With a flourish Ashil lifted the finished piece and handed it to Maggie for approval.

Maggie inspected the intricate embroidery, the delicate stitching on the fine cotton and expelled an envious sigh. "This is one of the most beautiful pieces of handwork I've ever seen, and I come from a long line of embroiderers." It was a pillow cover of deepest cobalt blue, with black lace trim, and gold stitching. "I mean it, Ashil."

Ashil blushed, folded it carefully and laid it aside. "Another one finished for Leslihan's hope chest."

Maggie surveyed the wool and needles in her lap. "The

chances are very good that all the camels in the yayla will be sold before I knit an acceptable sock."

Ashil laughed, stood up and shook out her apron. "That's possible." She gave a playful poke to the wool. "Yes, that's certainly possible."

☙

The days melded into weeks of sameness. Maggie developed an ease with Ashil, got a nod of acceptance occasionally from Ali as she helped serve the meals, or as he watched her make the bread and yogurt.

The children stopped to play with her and she knew all of them by name. They climbed over her when the women gathered to weave and spin, pointing out the difference between their dark skin and her fair skin.

The women had grown used to her presence. Many of them were still too shy to engage in conversation, but smiled at her at the spring, or when they gathered in the evenings to discuss the business of the tribe. She had expected more questions about her life, but soon realized they didn't know what to ask her, and didn't understand her life at all.

On occasion when she saw the chief, she stared at him directly, willing him to look at her. She wanted him to know she knew who had hurled those stones. To her surprise, he ignored her completely. Someone in the tribe welded a silent power, and Maggie hoped one day to know who it was. She took off her apron and folded it. "I've finished the milking and bread making. I'm off to my sitting spot."

Ashil smiled and nodded. "Don't forget to come back."

Maggie gathered up her scarf, a jug of water and two pieces of old carpet. She left the tent behind, looking over her shoulder before walking quickly up a path to a small knoll. In the shallow saucer of earth, soft grass was protected between two boulders. Maggie spread the carpets down. There was a slight incline for her head, and another for her feet. Lying down, she could turn her face to the sun, and yet be shielded completely from sight.

It was time to stop the obsession about things beyond her control. She was learning to deal with them when they came. She pushed up the sleeves of her blouse as high as she could above her elbows, unbuttoned the top two buttons on her blouse and tucked it in around her bra to expose fully her neck, pulled the legs of her şalvar above her knees, and laid back to soak up the sun.

In the distance she could hear the faint bleating of the sheep. A copper bell tinkled on someone's camel. She closed her eyes and welcomed the warmth. Just as the rays went from warm to hot, an unexpected spot of shade darkened the sky above her. Maggie squinted and saw Enver standing above her.

She flailed around to cover up. "Where did you come from?"

"Don't hurt yourself." He leaned on his staff.

"Why didn't you say something?" Maggie patted everything into place. "It's not fair to sneak up on somebody like that."

"I come this way every day," he said.

"You startled me," Maggie grumped. "I thought this was a safe hiding place."

"From what?" Enver asked.

"Not really hide, just get away. I'm tired." Maggie stopped herself. There was no need to complain. "I wanted to spend a few minutes by myself, to think in English." She motioned to the piece of carpet she was sitting on. "Really, I'm sorry. Sit down." Her mind flew to the last time she and Enver had sat together—the stars, the kiss, the heat. She felt a rush of blood to her face. She glanced at Enver.

He squatted down in front of her. The sun highlighted his black turban, his eyes, the strength in his jaw and chin. He spoke in English. "The last time we sat …"

"Don't say it." The flush on Maggie's face deepened. She didn't want him near her, didn't want to feel his heat, didn't want …

Enver looked straight into Maggie's eyes. "The man buying Ali's camel—"

"He's actually going to sell it?" Maggie interrupted in amazement.

"The man who is buying Ali's camel—"

"I can't believe it," Maggie interrupted again.

"Quiet," he growled. "It's important. The man's taking a truck back through our village tomorrow. If you want to go back, there's room for you." The furrow in his brow deepened. "He's taking his wife, too. Do you want to go back?"

Maggie's heart skipped a beat. She thought of the chief.

"Of course not," she said. "Before Leslihan's wedding? While I'm making friends with the women and learning how to dye carpets? I can't leave now."

Enver's black eyes revealed nothing.

"Do you want me to leave, is that why you're asking me?" She sucked in a breath. "Is this the chief's way of getting rid of me?"

"No one wants you to leave." Enver sat down and stretched his legs out. "As a matter of fact, the man who is buying Ali's camel told me he's been watching you and approved of how well you had worked with the women."

"He did, did he?" Maggie sniffed.

"Yes, he said he would consider you for his third wife—"

"What?"

"It's a little joke." Enver stopped Maggie from scrambling to her feet. "The reason I asked you is I thought you might be missing Haluk, and this would be a way for you to get back to Antalya."

"Or, you might be able to say that I wasn't tough enough to stay here," Maggie countered softly. "Or you want to win that bet with Haluk."

Enver plucked a handful of grass from between them. "You always think the worst." He held up a blade against the breeze. "Are you missing Haluk?"

Maggie was puzzled. "Yes, but I miss a lot of things. I miss Lahli and petting old Florence, lunch in the park and my suite, wait—I miss chocolate, actually—but that doesn't mean I'm ready to go back." Maggie studied him more closely. "I've worked hard here, done everything that's been asked, and I've still not been allowed to really learn to read the carpets," she leaned toward him, "and I'm not going back until I do."

Enver dropped the blade of grass. It blew in the breeze and landed on Maggie's knee. He looked into her eyes, at the sliver of grass, and slowly stood up without touching her.

Go ahead, I wouldn't mind.

He held out his hand. She hesitated, and then wordlessly took it. With an easy pull he stood her up at his side. "Haluk isn't the only one Mr. Beyter taught to be a gentleman." He smiled and left her standing with her jug and carpets. Maggie watched him walk toward the grazing sheep. He was everything Haluk was not. Serious, dedicated, dour even, but, she had to face the indisputable fact that something deep within her felt a kinship with him. That sense of aloneness, aloofness, that impenetrable barrier of self-protection needed to be breached.

༄

Leslihan's wedding was imminent and the excitement among the women was palpable. Rugs and pillows were piled around on the ground in front of Sema's tent. Today was the day the final items for Leslihan's hope chest would be given to her by the women. Then, she would display her trousseau carpet, the tangible proof of her prowess with the loom, and her value as a wife.

The skills a bride possessed were a form of currency, and the mother of a prospective groom could add much to her stable of daughters-in-law by selecting a girl with the abilities of Leslihan.

Leslihan sat in the middle of the women, basking in their attention. Maggie slid to the edge of the group. She wanted to watch this, and participate as a welcomed guest, but she was not a part of this clan, these close-knit women who held the tribe and a great part of its tribal standing together.

All of Leslihan's skills were evident in the stunning carpet laid out before them. The dominant colors of the Urek tribe, with its deep indigo blues, burgundy and meadow greens were the backdrop for the white camels, rams' horns, and flower motifs that showcased not only her expert weaving, but her attitude toward her expected abundant life. Leslihan glowed, and it showed in her trousseau carpet.

The women showered her with double layered white socks, knitted with knots of small flowers, special blankets and small prayer kilims.

"Maggie, come sit by me," Ashil said, on her way to make some tea. "We have a list of things to furnish Leslihan's new tent with, and Enver says that the man that bought Ali's camel is going back down to the village. We'll ask him to get her new milk cans and a copper tea pot."

"Please let me buy the milk cans or the tea pot," Maggie pleaded.

"But no socks from you," Ashil teased, and sat down with two glasses of hot amber tea.

Maggie smiled. "No knitted socks from me."

Later, in Ashil's tent, Ali and Enver sat smoking. Weddings meant visitors, and that meant lodging for them. Tents would have to be erected and the men needed information. The cool of the early night had settled in, and Maggie went to get her sweater. When she returned, Ali, Enver and Ashil were gathered at the small fire near the tent, drinking tea.

Enver spoke to her. "Ashil says the women have completed a lot of kilims, saddle covers, and prayer rugs to sell."

Maggie nodded. "I've seen them. At the proper market, they should bring excellent prices."

"Can they compete with the tribes who weave only for western homes?"

"Not in the same markets, but they shouldn't try. These pieces are art." Maggie sipped her tea, "Much too good for someone who doesn't understand the work involved or just wants a bargain."

Ali glanced at Enver. "Is she saying that our women shouldn't change?"

"I've never thought they should change their traditions and style of weaving." Maggie looked at Ali, who avoided her eyes. "They need to stop weaving for the cheap markets in Antalya, and let the people who would pay any price for their work buy them, or let Mr. Beyter' foundation buy them." Maggie stopped when Ali's eyes didn't register what she had said.

Ali spoke to Enver. "The chief still thinks she wants to corrupt them with change, and he only lets her stay here because of what Mustafa Beyter has done for our sheep."

Maggie steeled herself from screaming at the top of her lungs. *The chief stoned me and I'm still here trying to do what Mr. Beyter asked me to do!* Instead she said, "If he would just talk to me instead of about me he would know what I want to do is what Mr. Beyter wanted— to save this art and this tribe's history from dying."

Chapter Twelve

Maggie stood in the shade of Hala's tent. She blew out a breath of air that lifted wisps of hair off her forehead. Hot had arrived.

The small calendar back in her room was the only written indicator of the passage of time. She was amazed at how quickly she had regained her sense of listening to the cycle of the earth. The weather had hit its peak, she hoped. There would be a month of hot followed by the inevitable shaking off of summer as the earth slipped into the arms of autumn.

The days melded into seamless cycles of hard work, tempered by evenings of communal food and laughter. Maggie was surprised to find that Hala quietly wielded formidable power on behalf of the women. With her carefully chosen words, she commanded the attention of the men, generally one at a time, and never in the presence of the chief. He was the tribal leader, and that was an inviolate rule even Maggie had come to accept.

"Are you coming in?" Hala stepped to the front of her tent and tossed bread at a dog sitting nearby.

"Yes. Just stopped to realize I've been with you over three

months."

"Well, the almonds were green when you arrived, and we had sheared the sheep of their winter coat of wool." Hala thought for a moment, "Now it's the hottest time of the yayla, for a while, and then the air will change and we will go down the mountain. The almonds will be brown, the olives ripe and the sheep fat." She smiled with a deep satisfaction.

"When I was a girl, I could tell when autumn was coming by the sound of the wind in the leaves." Maggie took the tea. "I miss that."

"We need the seasons," Hala touched her chest, "It's medicine for the heart." She turned to go inside the tent. "And now we need to read my carpet."

Maggie followed. Stretched on poles in the middle of the tent, a large carpet divided the living area from her private sleeping room. This was not the same carpet from the village. This one was older and more worn. The light from the door and the light that filtered through the goat hair covering provided ample light for Maggie to see the hanging work of art.

Hala pulled up a small stool for herself, and Maggie rested on her knees in front of the carpet. Hala pointed with a gnarled finger along the bottom of the carpet, where the first rows of knots began to make a pattern. "This is the beginning," she said. "Here are the colors of my tribe, and my hopes for a good marriage." She pointed to the rows of deep green, black and cream colored geometric designs that Maggie recognized as hair bands. "This was my yearning to find a proper husband. He would marry me, take off my hair band

and comb my hair." She sat back. "Do you see that it is not the colors of my tribe today?"

"Yes." It was obviously not the burgundy, indigo and cream of the Urek tribe.

"Here is the falcon, the sign of my tribe, and here," she pointed to another row with a phoenix and a dragon fighting, "is the coming of the spring rain." She leaned over and touched an intricate design that to Maggie appeared to be the lazy *S* of a rancher's cattle brand. "That is my family motif. It is who I am."

Hala rubbed her hand over the carpet. "Here's where the mother of my mother wove a big ram's horn, see how big it is? Only a woman very sure of herself makes such boldness." She began to hum, and told the story of her life in the color and the motifs on the burnished woolen carpet.

Other women had knotted rows on the carpet, each one leaving a long thread as her signature. Maggie bent closer and saw countless threads, for the endless times a sister or cousin, friend or in-law sat and weaved on Hala's loom.

Maggie moved back to study the carpet. "This is a complete language. It is exactly why Mr. Beyter wanted you to keep weaving your history."

"When I was happy, I wove this red and when I was sad, or mad, I wove this black, black, black, for anyone to see." Hala sipped her tea and nodded. "I wasn't shy to express myself."

Maggie plunged in. "Hala, this lovely carpet, this story of your life, is why Mr. Beyter sent me here."

Intent on the carpet, neither woman heard nor saw a figure

standing in the door of the tent.

The chief spoke from the doorway. "It's hot today. I see you're reading a carpet." He stepped inside and Hala reached for a tea glass, filled it with the hot amber liquid and handed it to him unasked.

"I'm teaching Maggie to read my carpets," Hala pointed to another row of motifs, "You should listen, too."

The thunder built on the chief's face, but he kept his voice even when he spoke. "I haven't given you permission to speak to this American woman about our carpets."

"The sun is hot and the season is passing. When is the time to speak about these things?" Hala asked.

"When I'm ready," the chief said.

Hala scratched her head through her headscarf. "When will you be ready?"

Maggie watched the testy exchange between the wizened old woman and the smoldering chief.

"She's not proven herself to me." The chief glanced briefly in her direction. "She stoned our breeding ram."

"He's well enough." Hala stared pointedly at the chief, and then glanced back to Maggie. "She's working so hard she could be a nomad woman. What more does she need to do?"

The chief slowly set the tea glass down on the small tray. "Whatever I say. This woman being here doesn't change that."

He stalked out of the tent and the thud of a boot and a yelp from the sleeping dog split the air.

Stone the Goat

Of all the chores assigned her, dyeing the wool made Maggie feel in control. For at least that moment when she added the madder root, and watched the clear liquid turn burgundy, or when she poured ground indigo into water, and watched it bubble blue, she was a nomad woman, just as much as any that called this tribe their own.

Ali stood near her, his arms loaded with the dry red wool that was ready for Ashil to spin. Maggie added one last pile and tamped it down so he could see over it.

They both heard the tromping of heavy boots, and spun around to see the chief hurtling toward them. He stopped in Ali's face, wheezing, a fury barely contained.

Maggie held her breath. *What in the name of God had happened?*

Still panting, the chief stuck out his finger in Maggie's direction and his nose in Ali's face. "They're gone. All the sheep in the south corral."

"Gone?" Ali dropped the armload of dried red wool.

The chief trembled in barely contained anger. "Yes, gone. And *she*," he pivoted toward Maggie, "was the last one there."

Maggie stopped stirring. "What have I done?"

Ali's eyes pleaded with Maggie to remain silent. He hesitated then asked the question again. "What has she done?"

The chief, spittle forming in the crease of his lip, pointed his finger in a deadly aim at Maggie. "She left the gate to the sheep pen open last night."

Ali blanched and stepped backward unknowingly onto the pile of clean wool at his feet. "How do you know this?"

The chief drew himself up and glared at Ali. "It's enough that I know. The Saz have a sick herd, and if our flock gets mixed with them—where is Enver?"

"In the high pasture, he's been gone since yesterday." Ali kicked the wool aside. "He'll be back today."

The heat from the pot stung Maggie's eyes. The water bubbled unnoticed as she absorbed the accusation leveled at her.

"Get him. She's been nothing but trouble." The livid chief wagged his finger in Maggie's face. "You've had your chance. I fulfilled my promise to Mustafa Beyter." His eyes were slits of hate. He turned his fury once more on Ali. "Keep her here until Enver returns." He snapped at his dogs and churned the dirt as he barreled away.

Ali looked Maggie squarely in the eyes, his own pools of black in a drained face. "Where were you last night?"

"I went to water the sheep before dark. I thought the shepherds did all that but he told me to do it." She leaned on the stirring stick, oblivious to the pot that needed continual stirring.

"Who told you to go?" Ali asked.

"The chief. I was at Hala's. I took her some olives and bread. He came by and told me to go and water the sheep in the south corral," Maggie said.

"And then what?" Ali asked.

"I did it. I filled up all the troughs, and then I came home," Maggie said.

Stone the Goat

"You didn't close the gate?"

"Of course, I closed the gate." Maggie was adamant.

"He says you didn't," Ali said.

"Ali, I swear on a thousand camels I closed the gate. I am very careful with goats, you know that, and I've never been asked to take care of any of the sheep until yesterday." Maggie shook her head, "I don't know what more to say."

"I believe you. I have watched you work." Color returned to Ali's face, but the furrows on his brow deepened. "Ashil showed me the wool you dyed, you carry water in a steady way and your tea is almost good." Agitated, he kicked the wool out of his way, "But I have to find Enver. Go to our tent and wait there."

Maggie grabbed the wool Ali dropped and ran to the tent. She sat down on a bag of wool just inside and retraced her actions from the evening before. She had not left the gate open. She had left Hala's, went directly to the corral, emptied a dozen buckets of water from the barrel into the trough, watched the shepherd on the fence watching her, wondered why he wasn't doing it then fastened the gate and had come back to her room.

She sat glumly staring at the mountains. Today the peaks were ominous. The distant mountains no longer loomed as towers of strength. Somehow they had marched closer—the clenched fists of Allah thrust from the guts of the earth. Maggie's stomach burned.

She heard the scrunch of pebbles, and then her name. Enver flew into the tent. "What have you done?"

"I haven't done anything wrong!" Maggie felt her voice rising.

"I can't keep defending you." A certain weariness crept into Enver's voice. "And I don't have time to be responsible for you now. I've got sick sheep."

Maggie stood up. "I went to water the sheep because the chief asked me, I was careful and I did not, absolutely did not leave the gate open." Maggie spoke faster to make her point. "It must have been the shepherd sitting on the fence, the one watching me."

"Who was he?" Enver asked, "Let's go and find him, and I can go back to my sheep."

"I don't know. I haven't seen him before."

Enver shook his head and spoke slowly. "So, a shepherd watched you close the gate, but you've never seen him before."

"What do you want me to say, that I left the gate open? Maggie dropped down again on the sack of wool. "I didn't, and I am not going to take the blame for this." She hated the tears in her voice.

Enver pulled his turban off. "You'll have to leave, you know. I don't believe this, I can't believe this." He ran his fingers through his hair. "You'll be banished. The only truck going back left yesterday, with a sick woman from the Saz. There would have been room." He looked down at her sitting on the sack of wool. "How do you get into so much trouble?"

Maggie sprang up. "I don't know, it comes and jumps on me! Why would I make trouble for myself?"

"Stop whining," Enver said.

"I'm not," Maggie snorted.

"We have a problem with the sheep. I haven't told the chief yet. Some of the small tribes, for sure the Saz, have mingled their sickly sheep with ours and now, I have eight ewes I have to bring down from the far pasture." He sighed and rubbed the back of his neck. "I've got to go and get Dr. Lahli."

"You're going to Antalya?"

"Don't have a choice. Dr. Lahli will know how to take care of this immediately, but it will take five or six days to get her here, and I don't have room to take you because I need Reza and another boy to help me with the sheep."

Maggie was relieved. "I'm glad you can't take me. I don't want to go back. Hala says I have proven myself and she has read her carpets to me. She finally likes me." Maggie kicked at the bag of wool. "I have *earned my way*! Even Ali said I've done a good job. It's not fair. I swear to you I didn't leave the gate open."

"Many people like you."

"What?" Enver's change of tone startled Maggie.

"You said Hala finally likes you. A lot of people do."

"Do you?" It came out before she could stop it.

"Come here." His voice was deep and daring.

"Why?" Maggie's pulse quickened.

"Because I asked you," he said.

Maggie inched toward him. She stopped just out of reach.

"There's no one here." Enver took a step closer. "I'm leaving to get Dr. Lahli, and I want to kiss you before I go."

"What is wrong with you?" Maggie slapped the air between

them. "The chief thinks I've let the sheep out and …"

"You kissed me on the trip. It's only fair." He motioned her to him.

"A stupid mistake," Maggie said.

"You think it was a mistake?" He stepped toward her.

Maggie backed her way out of the tent into bright sunlight. "Hala says I have a smell of honor." She held out her hand to fend him off. "I have to keep my smell."

☙

Maggie stumbled from the front of the tent to her room at the rear, and fell through the flap into her small sanctuary. She might be able to handle the chief and the sheep and all the goats, but she couldn't handle Enver, not now. She sat on the carpets rocking back and forth, listening to the sounds around her. She would never belong here. No matter how many buckets of water, how many bags of wool, how much bread she carried, pounded or baked, the chief would make sure she never belonged.

Maggie stood up slowly. Deep in her gut, that pebble of courage she had found when she told Enver she was coming to the tribe was growing. She could feel it. It didn't matter that she would never belong here. What mattered was the two pots of water boiling away under her watch. Maggie wiped her face and adjusted her scarf. Neither the chief nor anyone else would deny these women their dyed wool, their colors, the only voice they had—if she could help it. They had worked too hard. She smacked the flap of her room open and walked quickly back to the pots.

Maggie paced and muttered. She stirred the water. Who was that shepherd? He looked like someone she had seen before. Where? He wore a brown vest with yellow stripes. Where had she seen those colors? The steam dampened her face. She focused on the bubbling blue water.

The man back in the village, the one that was trying to buy Ali's camel—took forever to do it—he had a blanket for his donkey with those colors. He was a Saz. No shepherd from another tribe would be so openly sitting on the fence when Maggie watered the sheep.

Maggie stopped stirring. "You naïve fool," she said aloud. "What better way to get rid of you."

Hala walked briskly up to the pots. "Time to see our colors," she smiled.

Maggie gave the pot a final stir. "Do you think this one is finished?"

Hala took the stick and gently moved it back and forth. She slipped some sand colored wool onto the stick, dipped it up and down, coaxing the dye to wrap the soft strands of wool in a deep blue embrace. She pulled it out and moved it directly into sunlight. She nodded her approval.

"It's very good. Our plants from last year dried well." She leaned on her stirring stick. "Some years when there isn't enough rain in the winter, the plants and roots give us a weak color, but this time," she stared into the water, "they're bright and bold. Like us."

Maggie's heart thudded in her chest. "The Saz use brown

and yellow for their tribe, don't they?"

"Oh, yes, that lazy bunch." Hala sneered. "When I married and came here, the old women in this tribe told me this. It isn't difficult to get a brown dye, and pointing to the masses of yellow flowers everywhere, "they don't work very hard for their colors."

Maggie pointed to the cluster of tents on a distant hill. "How long does it take to get over there?"

"Not long enough," Hala huffed. "They're not so good. I told the chief not to trade with them; their women can't knit or sew, and the cheese they make?" Hala wrinkled her nose in disgust. "Lazy nomads."

"If you're through with me, I need to do some work at Ashil's. I've been told I can only come here or be there."

"Yes, of course. Go now." Hala stirred the pot and sniffed the aroma of the dye. "It's good."

Maggie walked and half ran back to the tent. Ashil had gone with some of the women and children out to dig roots and would be gone all day. She searched for the large tribal scarf Ashil had given her, slipped it over her hair, brought it low on her brow and patted it into place. She was now appropriately covered. She slung the water bag Ashil had made for her over her shoulder and stuffed a few figs into her pocket. Outside she picked up one of Ali's walking sticks.

Maggie focused on her mission. When she had stoned the ram in the village, after he had slashed her bra and breast to within a hairs' breadth of her chest, she had said nothing to anyone. Enver let her stand in front of the chief and be vilified for her actions, because the chief didn't see a mark on her. She couldn't defend herself against the 'loose woman' title, and only Hala's goodwill had allowed her to participate in the tribal life. Now this—*this* was too much. For once she was going to take control and stand up for herself—let them see how a western woman handled a problem head on.

You shouldn't leave the tribe alone.

She hushed the voice inside and turned around carefully. She saw no one. She trotted down the path to the stream, turned back to the west, and followed a shepherd's trail around the tents and over the hill toward the Saz encampment.

Emboldened by her success that no one saw her leave, she made her way to the main path that connected all the tribes. Here, the grass was flattened by the hooves of thousands of sheep, dogs, and camels on their way around the vast valleys of the yayla.

For half an hour Maggie walked swiftly toward the tents, skirting the streams, following the meandering path. She topped another rise and found three shepherds sitting in the sun, eating. A fourth watched a small herd of scraggly sheep.

The biggest one, in a dirty yellow turban and motley brown socks stood in surprise, looking for the man they assumed was with her. "Who are you?"

"I have business with the Saz," Maggie didn't slow her stride.

"Then you have business with us." At his nod, the other two sprang up and stopped Maggie in the path.

The big one did the talking. "You alone?" He looked her

up and down.

Maggie jabbed the walking stick into the ground. "Yes, I'm alone."

The fourth shepherd had caught up, and they circled like hyenas, eyeing her.

Maggie stood still until the speaking one, scruffy, unshaved, and dirty stopped directly in front of her.

He looked at her scarf. "You're from the Urek tribe." He sniffed the air. "You smell like you need a man." He reached for Maggie's wrist. She jerked her hand away.

"Oh, some fun. She pretends to not want us. Who'll be first?" He looked around at the others.

Maggie didn't wait. She swung the walking stick with all her might at the talking man's head. It connected with a fierce whack. Be first and be fast—learned long ago from childhood taunts.

The big shepherd jumped back as blood from the blow spurted from his lip. Enraged, he grabbed Maggie by her neck and slung her into the tall grass. "Get the stick," he bellowed. The others swarmed her, clicking their tongues in a hypnotic frenzy, louder, louder. Dirty hands pinched her, clawed the stick from her hand. "Now beat her."

The smallest herder punched her in the face with both fists. Maggie screamed through the blinding pain when she felt the big man straddled her. She kicked in a ferocious instinct for survival, felt the flesh give way in his crotch and the primeval howl when he grabbed himself and fell in a writhing heap on the ground. He shouted for the others to grab her arms and

Stone the Goat

legs. "Beat her! Stone her!"

Maggie bucked and strained and wailed when two of them held her and the other one smashed his fist into her left eye. She shrieked. A searing pain snapped through her jaw and neck. She struggled to shield her face, but he punched her hard in the right eye—once—then again.

With a guttural moan Maggie kicked for her life. She gagged as their sweat sprayed her. They yanked her skirt up, and wadded it up at the waist. She screamed when a stone hit her cheek and screamed louder when a rock thudded against the side of her head. She prayed she would pass out before they stripped off her leggings. She heard the final rip and tear of her tunic and blouse, felt the knife blade against the bra—and then a slow breeze played on her exposed chest.

The four men recoiled. "Leave her! She's no good!" The fear she smelled now was not hers. They stumbled over each other in a frantic effort to leave. Dogs barked in confusion and a whip crackled in the air as they whipped their sheep and fled.

Maggie lay in a crumpled heap. Motionless, she strained to hear any sounds that they might be returning. All she could hear was her labored breathing. The sun warmed her face and moved slowly across the sky. A fly buzzed near her ear. She tried to swat it away. It landed on her arm and walked between the rivulets of blood drying there.

The earth moved, she must be dreaming. No, the earth moved as hooves thundered toward her. Maggie scrunched down further in the long grass. They were coming back.

"Maggie! Where are you?" Enver's hoarse voice carried over

the air. "I don't see her," he said to Ali.

Ali's fear was palpable. "They wouldn't take her! They must have left her somewhere!"

"Here, I'm here." Maggie groped for her blouse, struggled to sit up, but could not. She turned her face to the direction of the voices.

"Where?" Both men cried in unison.

"Here." Maggie raised her hand weakly. "Here."

She heard the rustle of the grass and felt the safety of solid arms as Ali and Enver lifted her up. They tucked her clothes around her and wrapped her in a blanket from Enver's camel saddle. Enver's smell filled her senses.

"Can you ride?" His voice was low.

"I can't see." Maggie's eyes were swollen shut.

Ali gently helped her onto the camel behind Enver. She put her arms around Enver's waist and laid her head on his back.

"Should we tie her to you?" Ali held out some rope to Enver.

"I'll be fine," Maggie mumbled before she toppled off the side. Ali caught her.

"Yes, we should," Enver said. Ali righted her and snugged the rope around her. "Here", he handed it to Enver. "Take her to Ashil. I'm going to the Saz."

Chapter Thirteen

MAGGIE LAY PROPPED on a feathery cushion of wool and soft carpets. She touched her face and the cotton turban of bandages that swathed her head. She focused on her hands, toes and finally Enver.

He sat on the floor near her bed, his knees drawn up to his chin, face pressed down on his folded arms. The exterior wall of the tent was rolled up, and anyone who passed could clearly see them.

"How long have I been here?" The words fell out of her mouth in a raspy garble.

"Two days," he said.

"You?" she asked.

"Same." He didn't look up.

Hot tears gushed in an unbidden torrent down her swollen cheeks.

"You were nearly raped, Maggie." Enver's voice cracked.

"I know," she whispered, plucking at the bandages on her hands.

"What stopped them?" Enver raised his head and scorched her in a single look. "What?"

"A ribbon of scar that runs in a straight stitched river across my chest wall," Maggie said.

"Yes," Enver said. "Yes." He caught her eyes and held them with his own. "A woman alone is a prostitute. That's been our law since ancient times. You know this, Maggie. Why would you test them?"

"I wasn't." Maggie swallowed hard. "I figured out the shepherd on the fence when the sheep got out was from the Saz tribe—he wore their colors. So why was he sitting on our corral?" Maggie spread her bruised hands in a helpless gesture, "To let the sheep out! So, I thought I could go to their encampment, find him, come back to the tribe and prove my innocence." Maggie stifled a sob.

"Ali found the shepherds. They're still hurting." Enver stood up.

"What did he do?" Maggie asked.

"He beat them with his staff, told them to go back to the high yayla." Enver paced back and forth in the small room.

"Did you find the shepherd in the camp?" Maggie hiccupped tears.

"There wasn't one. Ali looked everywhere," Enver said.

"There was, too," Maggie protested.

"It doesn't matter now. You have no idea what you've done." Enver sat back down and studied his socks. "You'll be banished. Out to the edge of the camp as soon as you're able."

Maggie shifted to her side, away from Enver. "I'm ready." The pain in Maggie's voice erupted from a place far beneath the bruises, the swollen arms and legs. "Take the sick sheep to Dr. Lahli. I'll do whatever and go wherever—."

"You can't go anywhere until you're well."

Maggie sat up and touched her mummy headdress. She wanted to go home, back to lay her head on her mother's lap, to listen to her hum an ancient hymn—back to Robert, to love him until the sweat filled sheets and the rhythm of their bodies rocked a child into her womb. "I should never have come."

Enver stood up, unfastened the carpet and rolled down the wall. "I should never have brought you."

☙

Maggie lay in the semi-darkness. She heard someone talking to her.

"Tea?" Hala's voice cut through Maggie's reverie.

"No, thank you."

"Drink it." Hala set the tray on the small table inside the flap.

"Where's Ashil?" Maggie struggled into a sitting position.

"Gone to get the others." Hala made herself comfortable on a small stool near Maggie's head.

Maggie breathed in deeply, the scent of wool, the smell of grass and earth, and the faint odor of something freshly cooked.

"I'm in a lot of trouble," Maggie said.

"Yes. But this is for us all to speak about. Drink your tea."

They arrived in a single group, the most influential women in the tribe. Maggie nodded to the ones she knew well, Tamay, Zeynep, and Sema. They all grouped around Maggie's bed, some on the floor, some with the stools they brought and Sema, with a giant pillow. None of the women had spindles. It seeped into her consciousness. Their hands were conspicuously still. The enormity of her actions loomed like a towering Oklahoma thunderhead on the horizon, a black roiling cloud as high and wide as she could see. There would be no shelter from this storm.

Maggie searched the gathering of somber faces and then fastened her gaze on Hala. The old woman loosened her scarf, adjusted it low on her forehead, wrapped it over her cheeks and nose, tucked it in on one side—pulled it tightly across her face in the opposite direction, denying Maggie all her face except the coldness of her eyes.

"You, Maggie Hanim, from America, have brought a great shame to our tribe. The bruises and cuts on your body are the marks from the Saz that you wear for leaving our tribe without a man. You deserved this beating."

Maggie had no idea what was beneath the swath of oatmeal colored strips of cloth that surrounded every limb. All she remembered was fighting off some drink that was so foul she hoped to die when Ashil forced it down her throat.

"Since the time of our mothers, and our mother's mothers, it is written that we will not travel alone. Our men cannot hold their heads up in the yayla, because you refused to obey our custom, and left our camp in secret; and the other tribes," Hala drew a large circle in the air, "think our men are so weak they cannot protect their own women. It's the worst shame."

"I realize," Maggie started.

Stone the Goat

"You realize nothing," Hala said. "For as many seasons as I have lived, we have had peace with all the tribes in the yayla. It is where we trade our goods and find the men our daughters will marry. And now, we, the Urek tribe," Hala sat up straight and tall, "the strongest in all of the yayla, must answer for allowing a strange woman to leave our camp without a man to guide her." Hala's eyes flashed with indignation. "You have betrayed us all."

Eleven angry women, their eyes shafts of hurt and bitterness, stared at Maggie, and drew their scarves across their faces in reproachful silence. Maggie's eyes flew to Ashil, but the scarf that covered her face could not cover the unbearable sadness in her eyes.

Maggie felt the hate pulsing around her, a white-hot hate that stemmed from her knowledge—she *knew* better than to leave the tribe, and had done so anyway.

"We welcomed you to our tribe and our homes." Hala twisted the end of her scarf into a small tight knot. "We taught you, we trusted you. You could have been a wife."

"But only a second wife," Tamay said quickly, "never a first."

"And now," Hala continued, "you'll go back to the village, and down to the sea; you'll leave us with the snickering of other men and women who say we should never have trusted an American." Hala leaned forward until Maggie could hear the immeasurable depth of pain in her voice. "Leslihan's groom might change his mind, the Urgaz chief might not want to do business with us. Why? Why would you betray us?"

Maggie sat mute in the bed. No one spoke, or moved. Eleven pair of expectant eyes bored into her.

"I didn't leave the gate unlocked." Maggie's chin trembled, but she forced her voice to stay strong. She could handle the physical pain, endure the bastard chief, but if these women turned their backs to her …

"I wanted to find the Saz shepherd and prove to the chief that I didn't leave the gate open because then I could stay here. I wanted to stay." Maggie did not try to stop the wash of tears that streamed down her bruised face and fell in hot splashes on her folded hands. "I wanted to do what Mr. Beyter asked me to do," she couldn't stop the hiccups and she didn't try, "because I've failed at everything else."

"There was no shepherd," Sema said. "Ali and my husband went to the Saz."

"There was. That's why I left the camp, to go find him. I had no reason to go the Saz otherwise, and I've never left before." Maggie trembled violently.

"There is a truth in this," Hala said.

Ashil spoke for the first time. "Why didn't you ask Enver to go with you? You belong to him."

"He wasn't here. He's with the sick sheep," Maggie said.

"Sick sheep?" Hala pulled on Maggie's sleeve. "How do you know this, where are they?"

'Enver told me he found some sheep and goats that didn't belong mixed with ours and they were sick, and now he has eight sick ewes." Maggie wiped her nose.

"The men have to take care of the sheep now, and then they

have to meet with all the tribes about you." Hala tapped her hand on the stool.

"Why do they have to meet about me?" Maggie dreaded the answer.

Sema snorted. "They may decide we aren't the best tribe in the yayla, our goods may not bring the best prices, and our daughters may not be offered the best husbands."

Tamay spoke for Ashil, who now sat pale and silent in the corner. "Because you went out alone our chief must ask forgiveness from the Saz chief because Ali beat their shepherds."

Hala glowered at Maggie. "This isn't easy for the chief to do. He and all the men in our tribe have been humiliated among all the tribes by a woman leaving our camp when they haven't done anything wrong." She stood up and reached for a stick. "We're going to find out about our sheep." With a cluck Hala dismissed the other women. She wagged the stick at Maggie. "You stay here."

Maggie sat in the shards of her shattered promise. All she had accomplished disappeared in the swish of the women's şalvars, the tightened scarves—the command from Hala. She sat unmoving until the light faded and the night crept in. Not one living thing crossed in front of her door flap. Not one child, not one dog, not one errant lamb. Maggie never stirred. If the wolves that sometimes raided the sheep passed her door tonight, they could feast on the woman within, the one who had never kept a promise.

Maggie listened to the muffled commotion. She moved slowly from her bed to the tent flap, teased it gently open and stepped outside. Trucks rumbled at the edge of the camp in the first light of morning. Diesel fuel permeated the air.

Maggie heard Enver and Ali as they came around the corner of the tent, followed by Reza and another young shepherd.

Ali motioned to the boys and they walked toward the trucks. "We'll get the water bags."

Enver stopped in front of her, a package in his hand.

"Just leaving, thought you'd still be asleep."

Maggie's mouth still hurt to talk. "Give this letter to Dr. Lahli before she comes or sends medicine."

"I will." Enver stood a moment longer, fingering the envelope. "Is there a cry for help in this message?"

"Read it. I've asked for a new compression sleeve." Maggie turned to step back inside the tent. "Don't follow me."

"Here." He handed her the package. "This is an old carpet from our tribe I found in Omar's shop in Antalya the day I drove you to the village." He lit a cigarette. "I always try to find the old ones and buy them back. They should be with us, not in some fancy dining hall of Europe."

"What's your point?" Maggie asked.

"You know a lot about our carpets. I've watched you at the looms with Ashil, and with Hala. Take it," Enver said.

"I don't know what's going to happen to me, but somehow I don't think I'll have time to study a carpet."

"For this week I'm gone, you're staying with Ashil and Ali

just like I promised you. Now take this, and read it, study it and then show Hala what you've learned."

Maggie threw him a weary look. "Why are you doing this?"

He turned away from her and back again. "I don't know." He ground the cigarette out under his heel. He stepped closer. "But I do know this, when I get back you're going to tell me why you kept that arm a secret."

Maggie rubbed her arm. It had gotten this large only once before in the years since her radical mastectomy.

☙

It wasn't hard to find the drunken man's home. One week to the day following Robert's funeral she parked at noon on the street in front of his house. She took Robert's baseball bat from the backseat and walked up the driveway. She stood transfixed at the sight of the old car and the smear of blood red paint from Robert's truck.

A slender woman appeared in the doorway with a portable phone in her hand. Maggie waited until a flash of recognition crossed the woman's face. Maggie steadied her stance and swung the bat with all her might. She started at the driver's door, moved methodically along the car, smashing every light, breaking every window and bashing every fender. She grunted in agony with every swing, sweat flying from her face, pain thudding in typhoon waves down her arms, legs and back.

The woman stood unmoving. When the pain doubled Maggie over and she couldn't catch her breath Maggie stopped and lifted her head. The woman stared at her for a long time, shifted her gaze to the car, then back to Maggie—still breathing hard. The woman held the phone a moment longer, dropped it into her pocket and closed the door.

༄

Maggie rubbed her arm again. "I didn't keep it a secret. I just didn't talk about it. Hurry up and get back here with Lahli," she said to Enver's receding figure.

In the five days since the beating she had spent most of her time in bed. Ashil, then Hala, had taken turns feeding her a drink so bitter she gagged. Maggie's left arm had remained swollen as other evidence of her beating faded. The removal of lymph nodes as a precaution to determine if the cancer had spread to the lymphatic system simply left the body with less ways to purify blood. Any number of things could cause the onset of swelling. It varied from woman to woman and and with degrees of severity. Whatever the case this time, Maggie was grateful for the bitter drink for it had worked. Ashil and Hala had helped her slide her arm into her compression sleeve.

The trucks finally rumbled away, headed to civilization. A place I should have never left, Maggie thought. The scent of pine wood smoke was in the air. The tribe was waking up. She stepped back into her small room and laid the folded carpet Enver had given her in the corner. Maybe later she'd try to read it, or maybe not at all. Now she would wait. Wait to get well, wait to get punished and wait to get banished.

Stone the Goat

Later in the morning Ashil called from outside her tent flap, "Hala wants to see you today, if you're better." Ashil was out of breath, buckets of water in each hand. She set them down and stepped into Maggie's room, then dropped down onto a thick pillow propped against the sturdy pole. "How do you feel?"

"Like a human again." Maggie offered a wan smile. She held out her arms, an ugly palette of bile green and putrid yellow, lifted her şalvar to reveal a similar pattern down both legs. Ashil had not forsaken her, and Maggie's heart had burst into happiness at the first tiny smile in the days following Hala's damning declaration. "Let me guess what my face looks like today."

"It's the color of camel dung around your eyes, and there are places as black as this tent near your nose and on your chin."

"Enough." Maggie shook her head as she searched the room. "Do you know where my breast is?"

Ashil reached for a woolen sack under the small table that held Maggie's kerosene lamp. She drew out a blue bundle and carefully unfolded it, handing the breast and bra to Maggie. "Here. When Enver brought you in that day, Hala and I washed you. Tamay helped us, and we put cloths on your bleeding and I had to explain what that," she pointed to the breast, "was." Uneasiness crept into her voice. "I didn't think you wanted anyone to know, but ..."

"This time I'm the one who understands," Maggie said, relieved. Now the whole village, assuming the women spoke to their husbands of such things, knew that she had been gored, and been vindicated in stoning the ram and why she hadn't been bloodied in the process.

Maggie slowly slid into her bra, and eased into her clothes. Finished at last, she picked up her scarf and covered her hair. "I'm ready." She took a deep breath.

"No." Ashil stood up and pulled the scarf over Maggie's cheeks and nose, tucked it on one side and crossed the opposite end just under her eyes and tucked it again. Only a narrow slit for Maggie's eyes remained.

"I can't show my face?" Maggie asked.

"No. You can't scare the children." Ashil patted the ends of the scarf in place.

"Look better?" Maggie asked.

"Yes." Ashil handed Maggie a spindle and a ball of wool. "Here, you can spin on the way."

Maggie lingered in the doorway. "I'm sorry I'm not well enough to carry water and do my part, and I am so sorry I have caused all this trouble."

Ashil leaned against the pole and said with a deep sadness in her voice, "Me too. Hala has talked with the chief and she'll speak for all of us. I don't know what he told her." She bent over and picked up the buckets. "Go."

Maggie walked slowly through the camp. There wasn't a spot on her body that didn't ache or hurt. She passed the tents where the young girls she had met sat on cushions, knotting

Stone the Goat

wool into endless rows of carpets, laughing with the others at looms set up under the same tree. They quieted when they saw her and turned away.

Hala sat in front of her tent. She threw some grain at the hens that pecked in the grass nearby. They squawked and fanned their feathers at Maggie's approach. She put her bucket down as Maggie approached. "Come sit with me. It's time for a glass of tea."

Maggie eased herself down on a flat kilim near Hala's stool. She reached for a handful of grain and tossed it toward the hens.

Hala handed Maggie a glass and wrapped her hands around a steaming glass of her own. She sipped and gazed toward the mountains; a thoughtfulness settling on her wrinkled brown face. She turned at last to face Maggie. The hens clucked contentedly between their feet.

Maggie sat unflinching as Hala's eyes roved over her. Then, Hala poured more tea and picked her teeth with a straw. She seemed to forget Maggie sat in front of her. She finally spoke. Her voice was a saber of steel. "You've caused many bad things to happen. Men have been beaten for something they don't understand, our chief has lost the respect of the other chiefs, and our women don't know if they can trust you anymore."

Maggie drooped under the weight of Hala's words. The only action that would be judged out of her entire stay would be this act of incomprehensible stupidity. "I will regret for the rest of my life leaving the tribe and what it has cost you. I had no idea all of this would happen." She swallowed hard. "I just wanted to prove that I didn't leave the gate unlatched, that I was worthy of your trust."

"You have lived in this country for several seasons, Enver tells me. How is it you don't know about traveling alone?"

"I do know. I thought just this one time I could—"

"Disobey our ways and follow your own? Doesn't work that way. This wouldn't have happened to you if you had asked a man to go with you." Hala shook her head slowly. "It's natural to want to find this boy on the fence and prove your innocence, but to go alone is asking to be used." She shook her head again. "I'm glad they didn't use you, but the beating you got for leaving this tribe," she stared deep into Maggie's eyes, "you deserved."

Maggie bit her lip. How many more times would she hear this? She inspected the bruising on her arm, the crusted scab on the puncture from the stone, felt the pain and pressure from her feet to the wound on her head. Maybe she did deserve it.

Chapter Fourteen

"I got it! I got it!" Maggie flew into the ramshackle house and grabbed her mother's hands. She pulled her into an Irish jig.

"What got did you get?" Ruth Meadows allowed herself to be jigged around the cramped space in the tiny room.

"The scholarship! From the Turkish man!" Maggie fell onto the small bed and fumbled the letter out of the envelope. "Here, read it." She watched her mother's face as she read the letter announcing Margaret Meadows would receive a full scholarship to the university commencing the beginning of the academic school year.

"I'm so proud of you, Maggie." Ruth hugged her tightly. "You deserve this."

"I can have some dreams now." Maggie couldn't stop smiling.

There had been many moments of dreaming, and most of them had come true.

This moment was not one of them. Maggie sat in the waiting room flipping through the years old magazines from the magazine rack. Her mother was in recovery from breast cancer surgery. A slow growing tumor, Dr. Denton had said.

The door swung open and a surgeon stepped out to speak to another woman in the waiting room. Maggie waited. For all the years she had worked for Mr. Beyter, she and her mother had done well, and been thankful … like now, for mammograms and the good insurance Mr. Beyter provided. The next surgeon out of the chute was the one she wanted to see.

He stood with her in front of the large window and gave her the news. "Your mother is fine. It was a slow growing tumor, like Dr. Denton said. We removed a substantial piece of her breast and several lymph nodes. It looks good. Don't let her skip any future appointments with the good doctor."

He left Maggie to process all she had heard. When she was called to her mother's room, she half ran down the long corridors to get there.

Mr. Beyter had been the best employer. He hired a private nurse to stay with Ruth Meadows initially, and then had an aide available for anything she would need when Maggie traveled.

Maggie was comforted to know her mother was incredibly happy with her circle of quilting friends, her community work and the small campus chapel services she regularly attended.

"All I want," Ruth Meadows said to Maggie months later, "is for you to come back if I get sick again."

"I promise you, Mother. I'll be back on the first plane home."

But that wasn't the way it happened.

Maggie had jetted off to Italy that month, not out of need,

Stone the Goat

no business involved, just a jaunt because she wanted to. When the call came that an undiagnosed fast-moving infection was raging through her mother's body, she had hurtled her way home, screaming through weather delays and late departures to arrive in time for a well-meaning nurse to say, poor thing, she asked for you, she did, there at the end, and with that sentence rent Maggie's heart in two.

☙

Maggie lifted her eyes to Hala. "I'd give anything if I could change what I did. There's so much I'd like to change, but I can't. I don't know what else to say."

Hala shifted on her stool. "Enver told the chief he's responsible for you."

She handed Maggie a handful of pistachio nuts. It was a small gesture of goodwill that Maggie accepted.

Several children panted their way past Hala's tent. They held bridles for donkeys and baskets for eggs. One stopped to offer Hala a string of figs. She ignored Maggie.

Hala took the string and waved them off. "We heard that Enver spoke up for you to the chief and said he would make it right with the other tribes. The men talked to him and then the women talked together and some of the women came to me."

"Who?" Maggie badly needed to hear someone was in her corner.

"Some women," Hala said. "I told them I smell truth around you now like I smelled honor before." Hala stood up and rubbed her hip. "Enver said that women lead easy lives beyond the yayla and are spoiled to softness. I think he is wrong at least some of the time. You've worked hard for us and you've suffered and never complained about it. Ashil told us about your breast, and why it's gone."

"What's going to happen to me?" Maggie dreaded the answer.

The old woman looked at Maggie with eyes a mixture of soft cotton and stone. Respect was there, and a resolve that punishment for a sin against the tribe would indeed be exacted.

"You will stay with Ali and Ashil until Enver gets back. After that you are banished from living with any of us. You have to go to the hut at the very edge of our camp and stay there until we go back to the village in the autumn."

"I deserve this," Maggie said.

"Yes, you do," Hala agreed. "Now you go and knit a sock. I'm watching you."

☙

Maggie sat with Hala and a group of women under a large pine tree. Some knitted, others worked their spindles, and the younger girls focused on intricate embroidery. Today was the day Enver was due back from Antalya with or without Lahli.

Sema basked in her elevated importance. The mother of the bride could direct this important event. "Who will cook the meat for the wedding?"

Hala chewed on a straw, "I'll roast the lambs and Maggie

can make the bread. We'll do it together."

Maggie released a small sigh of gratitude. Still shaken by her ordeal, her physical signs at least had healed. The attitude of the women had been cautiously accepting toward Maggie in the days since Hala had told them what her punishment would be. It was as if knowing she would be punished for her act of defiance had freed them to include her again. They no longer covered their faces in her presence and in groups of two and three stopped her to shyly ask questions about her arm and her breast. She had spent a lot of time reading in her Turkish dictionary to learn the words to best explain.

"When will the groom's family arrive?" Tamay asked.

"The men will come today and meet with the chief. His mother and all the family will be here tomorrow. They'll stay in the big tent beyond the corrals," Ashil said.

The women finished dividing various wedding feast preparations and strolled to the corrals to milk, leaving Maggie and Hala to cook the meat and bread for the upcoming feast.

Maggie sprinkled flour on the dough board and tested the domed metal plate for the right temperature. She knelt down and began to roll out the dough with the long dowel rod. She laid the flat piece of dough on the plate, it bubbled for a moment, and then she turned it for the final browning. She stuffed goat cheese and dried spinach between two pieces of the flat bread, and browned it once more on the hot plate until the cheese melted and the spinach softened.

She glanced up as a truck huffed its way past the edge of the camp, headed toward the corrals and the chief's tent. "I guess the groom has arrived."

Hala turned the skewered lamb slowly. "Yes. I recognize those colors." She smiled. "They will celebrate tonight."

The men climbed slowly out of the truck and surveyed the women walking by with spindles in their hands and buckets of water on their hips. Small children played hide and seek in the voluminous folds of their şalvars. Hens pecked the ground in search of a dropped crumb.

Maggie was near enough to admire their socks. They were sparkling white with wide green bands and cinnamon colored borders. A shepherd motif was on each one. The men had tucked their trousers into the long socks. "Those are handsome," she said.

"Yes, they are. That green comes from a garadal plant found in the west of the mountains. Their women search hard to get those colors." Hala spit out the straw dangling from her mouth. "Not like the Saz."

"I wonder what they're thinking?" Maggie said.

"The same as the chief. This is a good marriage for both tribes. We gain the right to more grazing in the yayla, and we become stronger than the others." She turned the spit and the lamb dripped fat into the fire.

Mountains of the still warm bread towered in a stack near Maggie. She could feel the moisture in the hollow of her back. The morning was getting hotter. She paused to wipe a sheen of perspiration from her face.

She heard footsteps and saw the three pairs of Urgaz socks walking by. Maggie shaded her eyes and studied the backs of the three men as they passed through the camp. The youngest one glanced back at her.

It can't be. The boy on the fence.

Maggie saw them stop to talk to Ali. She stared at them. At him. Maggie quickly filled two large baskets with the treat. "I'll be back in a minute." She adjusted her scarf, and walked slowly toward them, carefully holding the baskets piled with food. When a whiff of the hot bread reached them, they all turned toward her.

Maggie stared at the young boy in the middle.

He was the shepherd who was sitting on the fence the day the sheep got out of the corral. He was wearing colors from the Saz that day.

Maggie's heart thudded. She kept walking. It just wasn't possible. It was possible. He had recognized her. She stopped at the edge of the tents. "But he's an Urgaz," she said aloud to give some sense to her racing brain. "He's here—Leslihan's groom—Urgaz colors. Maggie watched them until they entered the chief's tent. She walked slowly back to the outdoor kitchen.

Maggie pieced it together in her mind. What if the chief had paid someone to disguise himself as a Saz shepherd, to open the gate and let the sheep out? If she could get blamed for that he could banish her for it. But this banishment was really for standing up to him when she was getting water and, well yes, for insulting him to his face.

Hala sat on the small stool and turned the meat. Fat fell into the fire, and the smell of the roasting meat caused Maggie to pause. A drop of fat fell to a sizzling death.

"How long before that meat is ready?" Maggie asked.

Hala sliced off a thin strip, looped it over the long knife and handed it to Maggie. "Taste."

Maggie slid the thick strand into her mouth all at once. The slight crunch of the seared piece melted in an explosion of spicy flavor. For a moment she forgot the boy. "Good." She licked her fingers.

Hala smiled, "A lifetime of cooking."

A flurry of excitement swept the camp as a second truck could be seen in the distance.

"Do you think that's Enver?" Maggie stacked the bread and tried to focus on her job.

"I think so. Watch yourself, you're burning the bread." Hala stood and yawned. "It's a good time in the yayla." She lifted her face to the sun, "A time for celebration and happiness."

Maggie stood on her toes and strained to see if the truck, which had stopped at the far end of the village, was Enver's. Was Lahli with him? She couldn't tell. She knelt back down to the fire. The sheep weren't stolen, for sure they were hidden somewhere and Maggie would bet anything that at the appropriate time would be found. If she hadn't gone to the Saz, the chief would have sent her down the mountain on that last truck and she wouldn't be here now.

Shouts came from the women gathered at the trucks and a voice rose above the others.

In a moment the crowd parted and Maggie saw a tired and rumpled Dr. Lahli move toward her. Maggie gave a half-hearted brush to the coat of flour that covered the sweat and willed herself not to dash toward Lahli. She stood and allowed her to initiate the greeting.

Lahli kissed Maggie's cheeks and held her out for an inspection. "You look like a nomad woman." She drew her close and adjusted Maggie's scarf. "I'm glad to see you." She draped her arm around Maggie's shoulders. "You have a lot to tell me. Let me get settled and pay my respects to Hala, and the chief. We'll have a very long chat."

Maggie sat down at the pile of bread. Lahli was here. She was no longer alone. Moisture pooled in her eyes and a single happy tear slid down her smiling cheek and dropped in a warm splash onto her hands.

※

"Hello." Maggie stood outside Lahli's tent door.

"Come in." Lahli reclined on tribal pillows. She fished a dark olive out of a small bowl and motioned Maggie to join her on the soft thick carpet. "Sit here and let me look at you."

Maggie complied. She sat cross-legged in front of Lahli.

"Hold out your hands, palms up. Now look up and let me see your face."

Maggie leaned forward and held her hands out for inspection.

"Calluses." Lahli scrutinized Maggie's palms. "A sign of hard work that I can see. Tell me about things I can't see."

A torrent of emotion surged through Maggie. "I don't know where to start. What has Enver told you?"

"That you had earned the respect of the women, and most of the men and lost it all in a secret trip to the Saz."

"I never made it there."

"He told me that too." Lahli rubbed Maggie's hand in her own. "Why did you leave here to go there alone?"

"I don't know. Yes, I do." Maggie pulled her hands away, balled them together in front of her chest. "The chief accused me of leaving the gate unlatched, and I didn't. There was a boy, sitting on the fence, just sitting there watching me, from the Saz tribe. Then the gate was opened and the sheep were gone." Maggie spread her hands. "I know in my gut he opened the gate."

"And you went to find him? "Lahli asked.

"Yes. And you know the rest. The chief said that some of the sheep got mixed up with others that were sick, and then Ali beat the shepherds and now I'm banished to the edge of the world. There are wolves out there, and then … I don't know." Maggie twisted her şalvar between her fingers. "I went to find this shepherd. What a mistake."

"Yes, a costly one." Lahli sat back against the pillows. "And not just for you. Reza told me Enver stood in front of the men and told them he, not the tribe, was responsible for you, and he would go to all the chiefs throughout the yayla, accept the full blame for the foreigner in their midst, and pay whatever the cost to the shepherds Ali beat."

Maggie clapped her hands over her ears. "Don't tell me this. Hala said the same thing, and I can't stand it!"

"Yes, you can, and you will. Why would he do that?" Lahli's voice was soft, but insistent. "Do you know why he would do that?"

"Because he places the tribe above his own feelings," Maggie said, "and he's an honorable man." Somehow the sight of Enver, begging, on her behalf, in front of the chief, hurt more than all the stones she had endured.

"Yes, but more." Lahli sat up straight again. "He did it because he believes you are succeeding. He listens to the men in the tribe, and they talk about how hard you work. They listen to their wives, who tell them you can't knit but you are very good at milking, that your bread is good and your tea is getting better."

"Are you telling me that I have a chance to make this work?" The possibility of success was so far removed from Maggie's thoughts she couldn't grasp the notion.

"Had a chance. Who knows anymore. But you should know what Enver did for you, either way."

Singing and the sound of a flute filled the air. "We'll talk later, but now," Lahli stood and stretched, "I think Reza and his flute are calling. Come, let's go and listen to the pre-nuptial celebration."

"I'm not allowed to go anywhere, Lahli." Maggie sat in a listless slump.

"I don't need the chief's permission." Lahli bent over and rubbed Maggie's shoulder. "He isn't going to say anything if you're with me."

A small voice spoke from beyond the tent flap. "Are you coming out to eat with us?" Maggie pulled it open and saw a tiny girl with giant almond eyes. "Hala says she's ready and won't wait until the moon comes up. Hurry." The child skipped off toward the scent of roasting lamb.

"We're on our way," Maggie spoke to the retreating figure.

☙

"Well, what a day." Lahli dropped down onto the floor of the tent and held out her tea glass to Maggie. "Pour me a bit of that elixir of life."

Maggie had spent the day marveling at the Lahli machine in action. First, all the men and boys had rounded up the nearer flocks of sheep and goats and herded them through the corral. Enver and Ali held them while Lahli expertly inoculated each one in a concerted mass effort that left the tribe in awe of how quickly it could be done. Shepherds had been dispatched to bring the other animals to the corral.

Maggie had delivered basket after basket of yogurt soup, bread and fried meat, walnuts, pistachios, and figs. Sema had set up a şamovar to make tea, and the trio of Lahli, Enver and Ali stopped only to eat and rest a few minutes before wading into the woolly fray again. It had lasted until late evening.

Maggie filled the glass. "How many sheep will you have to inspect after the wedding?"

"None, we did it all today." Lahli stretched her legs out and leaned back on the thick pillow. "I stopped doing this kind of thing years ago. It's why I have a staff."

"I wondered why you came yourself. I know how busy you are." Maggie laughed wistfully. "I remember my life before this trek, and you were in it."

"I came because Enver asked me," Lahli said. "He knows enough about animals to know when they're sick and can be treated with local salts and minerals, but if he says there could be an epidemic of something, I come myself." Lahli sighed. "There's never enough time—but always time for this." She raised her glass in a toast. "Besides, he's worried about you."

"He's afraid I'll do something stupid again," Maggie said.

"Because," Lahli sipped, "he worries that you won't abide by the tribal customs, and he can't deliver you safely back to Haluk as he promised. He doesn't need to worry about that anymore, does he?"

Maggie thought of Leslihan's groom who would be here until the wedding. She hesitated.

"Tell me he doesn't have to worry about you leaving again." Lahli sat straight up. "This is not acceptable, Maggie. I'll defend your right to stay here, but only if you promise me that you will not go out alone again." Lahli was not smiling.

"Do you think I did the wrong thing by going to the Saz alone?" Maggie's voice trembled at the memory. "Did I deserve to get beaten?"

"You shouldn't have gone alone. If you want an ally in this it won't be me." Lahli leaned forward and cupped Maggie's face in her hands. "There are two Turkeys: no, countless Turkeys, just like there are countless Americas. You have to abide by local law wherever you are."

"Meaning what?"

"I have a French friend, you know her, Gisele and she told

me—"

"What has that got to do with me?" Maggie yelped.

"Everything. Listen." Lahli sat back. "Gisele was on holiday in America, I don't remember where, and she took off her bathing suit top to lie in the sun. Someone told her to put it on, she asked why because she sunbathed this way in all of Europe—"

"I still don't see what this had to do with me." Maggie wasn't interested in Gisele's little nipple problem.

"Yes, but listen, a policeman arrived and told her to dress. Gisele did what Gisele does, she refused and what happened? She was taken to the prison in handcuffs! Locked away!" Lahli waved her hands as she spoke. "She was incensed! How could this happen? She has a prison record, and she hadn't committed a crime."

"It's not the same," Maggie said quietly.

"It's the law and the custom of the land," Lahli replied.

"And it wasn't a prison, just jail. And it was a misdemeanor, not a felony." The words sounded hollow to Maggie.

Lahli continued with a sense of urgency. "Gisele knows not to go alone out at night in any big city. She understands what might happen to her, but she couldn't understand the problem of tanning without a top." Lahli paused. "I said to her what I say to you—*abide by the law of the culture you're in.*" Lahli pushed her glasses up on her nose and collapsed against the pillow. "So, there you have it."

Maggie looked backward, back into her years traveling the width and breadth of Turkey. She had never encountered anything like what had happened to her. Anywhere. This was a harshness she knew existed on some level, but had spectacularly failed to grasp its consequence.

"Would they have raped me?" Maggie asked softly.

"Those men would have, yes, others from more respected tribes, no," Lahli said.

"Why didn't they? It was a long time before Enver and Ali got there." Maggie said.

"Probably superstition. Whatever made your breast fall off might make their manhood fall off, and that, dear girl, will kill desire in even a wretched man," Lahli said.

Maggie picked at a strand of wool in the carpet. "Saved twice by a breast I don't have." She shivered uncontrollably at the thought of the giant ram, thrusting his horn into her prosthesis and missing her chest by a hair's breadth … shivered as the smell of the Saz shepherds flooded her senses.

She stared at Lahli and opened her mouth to speak, but didn't.

"What is it? Tell me what's on your mind," Lahli said.

"You're not going to believe this," Maggie said.

"Tell me anyway."

" Leslihan's groom, the one that's here right now, was the Saz boy sitting on the fence the day the sheep got out and—"

"What?" Lahli shook her head.

"I knew you wouldn't believe me." Maggie drained the tea from her glass.

"I didn't say that. Are you sure?" Lahli sat straight up again.

"Yes. I recognized him earlier when he and his entourage

arrived for the wedding. And he *knew I knew!*"

"Why in the world would he do that?" Maggie asked.

"What do I do?" Maggie struggled to keep her voice from rising. "Am I supposed to let all the tribes in the entire yayla believe, first, that I'm a loose woman, and now, that I can't be depended on to latch a gate? The chief is behind all this. He wants to get me into so much trouble no one will listen to me. He got this new groom-to-be to sit on that fence with the Saz colors." She jumbled her words. "This way I would blame a Saz shepherd, and I'll bet a year's salary that the damn sheep are somewhere around here."

"How is this possible?" Lahli asked the oil lamp sitting in the middle of the room.

༄

The drums began to beat. A flute sounded, and laughter fueled by visiting men and much raki swept in waves from the gathering of men near the fire pit.

Regardless of the tumult in Maggie's mind, there was a wedding tomorrow and a henna party for Leslihan tonight. Lahli had said she could go. She left Lahli and ran quickly back to her room. Ashil had left early to help Sema prepare, and Ali was with the men. Maggie slipped on a long blue skirt, white blouse and dull gray vest. She wrapped a grey scarf around her head. The lower the profile she kept, the better off she would be.

She ran back to Lahli's. Just being with Lahli was a balm to her soul, and she had no intention of missing a moment of

Stone the Goat

their short time together.

"This will be fun," Lahli said. She wore a long brown şalvar covered in white orchids, a peasant blouse of faintest pink, and a darker pink shawl. Her white hair was tucked into a loose chignon. "In Antalya we know this isn't necessary," Lahli said as she slipped a white chiffon scarf over her hair, "but I will do it here out of respect for my tribe." Lahli smiled gently at Maggie.

They walked side by side toward Sema's tent. "Fresh air will help us clear our minds."

They passed the group of men, sprawled on kilims, some sitting on their haunches, faces reflecting the firelight. Small dots of red light glowed from cigarettes and laughter floated on the air. The drum beat pulsed through the camp, and Maggie glanced furtively at the group. Enver sat between the two chiefs, a glass of raki in his hand, his head tilted toward the visiting chief. Maggie jerked her eyes away.

Maggie focused on the softness of Lahli's face, the contentment radiating from her body. "You could be the bride."

"I've been the bride, and the wife and now the widow." She put her arm around Maggie. "We are the same, yes?"

"Yes." Maggie tightened her grip on Lahli's waist. "You told me once you were happy in your marriage. Would you ever want to marry again?"

"I was happy. Did I tell you I met my husband at Bilkent University in Ankara? He was all dressed in his military uniform, and I melted like the soft cheese tucked inside a piece of bread. So handsome, and of course, I wanted his attention."

"You never told me that!" Maggie said. "Did you flirt with him?"

"Well," Lahli smiled, "we didn't call it that."

Several other women caught up with them and they walked in a seamless flow to Sema's tent. All of the women, young girls and laughing babies were gathered together, eating cakes and drinking sweet milk. Maggie and Lahli stepped carefully between them to sit in the middle near Ashil.

Sema, the proud mother took command of the group. "It's time to bring Leslihan out." There was a rustle in the other room of the tent, and a giggle as the thin kilim that served as the door was opened by one of Leslihan's cousins. She pointed to Tamay. "Put the lights out."

Ashil extracted an onion and a short knife from the folds of her şalvar. She quickly cut the onion in half. She wrapped each halve in a handkerchief and handed them to Lahli. "Pass this around to Sema."

Lahli scooted around two women and tugged on Sema's şalvar. "From Ashil," she whispered.

Sema recognized what she had been given and nodded thanks in Ashil's direction.

Lahli moved back to her seat, as the room went black and an excited murmur raced around the group of women.

"What was that for?" Maggie whispered.

"Sometimes the bride gets too excited to cry. This onion guarantee tears." Lahli whispered back. When their eyes had adjusted to the darkness, four of Leslihan's cousins entered the room holding candles. Leslihan, in a shimmering nightgown followed.

The light from the candles was enough for Maggie to see the fine embroidery, the translucent cotton and the pink scallops. The transparent veil did not hide Leslihan's lovely face.

Leslihan was helped to a seat on a red silk cushion in the middle of the room, and Hala and Sema stood before the group of expectant faces.

Hala spoke. "This is the first important day in the life of Leslihan. From this marriage she can bear the children, the strong handsome sons to care for her in her old age and daughters to teach the skill of weaving and how to keep a proper house. And now I will tell you the poem of sadness and joy which will be the marriage vow."

The singsong voice of Hala cast a spell on Maggie. How many times had she recited this, Maggie wondered, how many young women had left their homes, to go and live somewhere else, to be absorbed into the fabric of someone else's life, to change, make do, to adapt?

Sema knelt down and opened the veil. She wept, copious tears, and wept more at the sight of her daughter who would, in the light of the next new day, go to live with another tribe and become the daughter to another woman. She held Leslihan tightly, and Leslihan mixed her tears with those of her mother. The sadness was contagious, and Maggie blew her nose and wiped her eyes before Lahli and Ashil did the same. Every woman and girl in the room watered their hands with the salty tears of goodbye.

Hala ended the poem. The women dried their eyes and

sat quietly as Sema, with great care, took the pot of henna and painted a decorative pattern that covered Leslihan's arms and legs. The sight of Sema, leaving the marks of a mother's love in each stroke of the fine brush caused Maggie's throat to close, and the tears that fell this time were for herself, and her mother, in another time and place.

When Sema finished, she took long cotton strips and began to bind Leslihan's arms, legs and feet to soak up the henna. She handed the pot to Zeynep, who took the brush and dabbed a bit of the henna on her hand. One by one the women in the room accepted the pot, performed the simple ritual and passed it on.

"What am I doing?" Maggie whispered to Lahli. She placed a dab on her hand and passed the pot.

Lahli took her time and stroked a smidge on each hand. "You're wish is for Leslihan to have good luck in her marriage."

When the pot had been returned, Sema produced a gold coin and bound it in Leslihan's right hand. Sema stood and smiled at the women sitting around her. "We can go now. She'll be safe here until tomorrow."

Maggie and Lahli left the tent and the group of cousins and friends who would remain with Leslihan. They breathed deeply of the cool night air. They bade their goodnights to the women and wandered to the edge of the camp where the camels sat resting for the night.

"What happens now?" Maggie asked.

"Tomorrow Sema will unbind Leslihan, and the henna will

Stone the Goat

have softened and darkened overnight. It will last a long time. I promise you she will be beautiful. The groom gets the coin for good luck." Lahli absently toyed with the gold bangles on her arm. "You asked me if I would ever marry again." She turned her head toward the dark night sky. "I don't think so. I've made a life for myself at the university." She shivered in the air. "One good marriage is enough. And you?"

Maggie's life with Robert flashed before her eyes. Her wedding had been held on a clear October day, with Mr. Beyter standing in for her father at the quiet service in the campus chapel. He had offered her a huge affair, she had declined. She and Robert had gone camping in the eastern Oklahoma woods and she had come home with poison ivy on her bottom. "I had the happiest years of my life with Robert. I don't think I could ever have that again."

Lahli reached for Maggie's hand. "You're still a young woman. Perhaps the henna will be good luck for you."

⁂

Maggie slept fitfully. Dreams of Robert wearing a turban, Mr. Beyter playing a flute and her mother dancing around in a white veil all clamored for attention. She was relieved to see the dawn.

Hala came early. "The chief says you can't come to the wedding."

"Why am I not surprised?" Maggie's steeled herself against the disappointment.

"You're not a nomad and you don't belong to a tribe." Hala

wore an exquisite white scarf, with tiny embroidered flowers of pink and yellow sewn to the edge. Her leathery face was shiny in the morning sun. "And the groom doesn't want you." With that she left as quickly as she had arrived.

So this was the beginning of her punishment. She had been to other weddings. The bride would prostrate herself before her mother-in-law to be, show off her extensive hope chest of items and kiss the hands of all the women present.

She heard the men dancing, the drums wild with the beat of a new marriage underway. The men would be sticking money on the sweaty brow of the groom, and his cohorts would prepare a cart for Leslihan, beautiful in her red bridal finery, to ride to her new home.

When the feasting was over, Maggie stood in the opening to her room. Through the trees she saw the procession of donkeys, camels, children, women and men form a slow snaking curve out of the camp and up the small rise in the direction of the Saz encampment. Somewhere beyond lay the Urgaz camp where Leslihan would become the property of her groom tonight and mother-in-law tomorrow.

Chapter Fifteen

It was dawn of the morning after the wedding. The truck that would take Lahli back to Antalya stopped a few feet from where she and Lahli were standing. Maggie set two buckets down near her feet. She would get water as soon as Lahli was on her way.

"I think you need to give your arm a rest," Lahli said. "I'm worried about you. I wish I could take you back with me but the chief won't let me. Do you want to come back to Antalya with me?"

A surge of homesickness surged through Maggie. Of course, she did. She wanted sameness, familiarity, friends, days with Haluk and nights with Lahli, or maybe she wanted the last two things in reverse.

"Yes. I want to get a manicure like yours, spend two days in a hot shower, polish my toe nails and eat fresh fish." Maggie picked up her buckets. "And no."

She couldn't articulate her need to stay—at loggerheads with the perfectly sane reasons she should go. The promise to Mr. Beyter was no longer the single driving force. She needed to stay until the women understood her. She longed for their approval and respect.

Lahli stood quietly for a long moment. "So, eating dried figs, pounding wool, carrying water, and sock knitting wins over a hot shower and a feather bed?"

"Who told you about my knitting?" Maggie asked.

"Everyone," Lahli smiled at her over her glasses. "Please obey the chief. I'll see you in a few weeks." Lahli picked up her medical bag and handed it to the driver.

"Will you be my first dinner date when I get back?" Maggie asked.

"You prefer me to Haluk?" Lahli smiled.

"He's too busy for me. It would take him a week to clear his calendar."

"Do you know why Haluk never asked you out?" Lahli paused with her hand on the truck handle.

"Sure. He likes those leggy models from Europe, the ones that hang all over him. I've seen him at parties in Istanbul when I was there with Mr. Beyter."

"I don't think you knew that Mustafa threatened him if he so much as looked at you as long as you were in his employ. I actually was at a dinner when Haluk asked to take you to the opera in Antalya, and Mustafa just laughed and said, 'go find yourself another woman'."

Maggie felt the flush climbing up her face. She hoped Lahli didn't notice. Was it possible?

"Don't forget these people are my people, even the chief," Lahli said.

Maggie took both Lahli's hands. "I won't. I know what you've done for me. I won't forget it."

Stone the Goat

Lahli shook her head slightly. "You'll never know what I've done for you. It would take twelve generations in my culture for you to understand, but I do it because you are my friend, and out of respect for Mustafa Beyter."

The driver coughed. The tribe had said their goodbyes to Lahli the night before. She climbed into the truck and waved to Maggie as they started in a smooth roll east toward the sunrise.

☙

No one else was up. All the reveling had worn out the entire tribe. Maggie picked up two buckets and headed toward the stream. A good walk would do her good, and Ashil would be pleased with fresh water. She hesitated at the sound of two voices, and quickly stepped around the back side of a boulder and slid to the ground. A tall stand of yellow flowers gave her added cover.

Reza and the chief were on the path headed toward the camp. Reza was breathing hard. "I saw the sheep, all of them. They're in a corral near the Urgaz tribe." He caught his breath. "I tried to tell the shepherd they were ours but he said it wasn't true."

The chief growled. "Those don't belong to us. That woman turned our sheep loose, and we'll never get them back."

"But I saw our mark." Reza was insistent.

The chief stopped just beyond Maggie's rock. She scrunched further down. "No," he said. "They're not ours. Don't mention it again. Let's go."

I knew it!

Maggie held her breath until they were well out of sight. She waited until she couldn't hear them and raced down the path with water spilling out of both buckets. She dropped them near Ashil's cooking pit and flew into her room with her fists in the air. Soundlessly she punched and kicked and fought a foe that only she could see. A small pillow sat on the pile of sleeping carpets. Maggie grabbed it and threw it on the floor, dropped onto her knees and pummeled it. The stitching gave way, and Maggie beat it until the last bit of innocent wool floated upward in total surrender. Fully spent, Maggie lay sprawled on the floor in the fluttering wool. *I knew it.*

Minutes later she heard the chief stop in front of the tent and speak to Ali. "Take that woman to the hut today. I don't want to see her. She eats alone."

Maggie heard his footsteps fade, listened to Ali and Ashil murmur heatedly, and then heard them leave the tent together.

A rooster crowed just outside her door and startled her. She opened the flap and whooshed him along his way. She heard Ashil and walked around the tent to see Ali park a small wooden wheelbarrow. Ashil had a large bundle in her arm. "I'm sorry Maggie, but it's time to go to the hut."

"I'll get my things." Maggie returned with the pillow under her arm and a duffel bag in each hand. She loaded the bags into the wheelbarrow. "May I take this pillow?" She had tried unsuccessfully to repack the wool.

"Please, take it, and the sleeping carpets." Ashil quickly

gathered them up and stacked them high on top of Maggie's bags.

With Ali pushing the wheelbarrow, the three of them walked through the maze of tents, out past the small plot of grass where visiting donkeys and camels grazed, and to the old shepherd's hut at the edge of the corral. It squatted in the shadows of a thick stand of yellow pines.

They unloaded the wheelbarrow. Maggie glanced around at how she would spend the end of her days in the yayla. After months of work, the mental exhaustion of speaking in another language all the time, and an on-going battle to keep her arm under control—this was what she had to show for it.

The hut was somewhat larger than the small room at Ashil's. Ali stacked the sleeping carpets against the stone wall in the back. Maggie set her bags on the worn kilim on the ground. There were no windows, just the door opening and the light that filtered through the woven branches holding up the goat hair covering.

Ashil opened the bundle. "You can use these." She set a metal pan and a water jug down, "that's from Hala;" a small iron pot with a spoon, "that's from Zeynep;" a tin plate and a fork, "that's from Tamay;" one glass for tea and a şamovar for making it, "and that's from me.

"Hala will come when the sun sits on top of that peak." Ashil pointed to the nearest mountain. "The chief says you can't be with us in the evening." She glanced at Ali who was filling the wheelbarrow with limbs that had fallen from the pine trees. She fidgeted in front of Maggie. She reached into her apron and handed Maggie a second glass and whispered, "He didn't say we couldn't come to see you."

Maggie clasped the glass to her chest. "Come back," she whispered back. "Please."

Ali pushed the wheelbarrow filled with limbs to the path and turned back to Ashil. "It's time to go."

"Thank you both for bringing my things here," Maggie said, gratitude welling up inside her.

"Be careful." Ashil patted her hand. "I know you will." She joined Ali and they walked side by side until a curve in the path and a thick grouping of trees shielded them from view.

Maggie walked around the hut and listened … nothing. For the first time in four months she was actually alone. She could make her meals, boil her tea; do whatever she wanted.

She walked a few paces from her door and glanced into the corral. There were no sheep or goats milling around. This was where the shepherd had sat on the fence when the sheep had disappeared.

Maggie checked the flap of the door. It was heavy felt, the kind of felted wool used for centuries to keep the rain off shepherds or to keep the tent floors dry from wet ground underneath.

It wouldn't keep an animal out, but she could gather some large stones, get a stout limb she could make into a walking stick and be prepared.

She noticed the position of the morning sun. She had time to collect firewood before Hala arrived. She could get water later. She didn't have a metal dome to make bread, but surely

Stone the Goat

the chief wouldn't deny her bread. Surely.

Maggie reached for the leather straps hanging by the door and headed to the grove of pines behind the hut. She gathered small twigs to use as kindling, and thin branches and small limbs to heat the water for the şamovar. These could be used for the bread dome, if she should be so lucky as to get one. She wrapped the leather straps around the bundle and hefted it to her shoulder. She was steps away from her door when Enver approached with a portable loom used to make kilims.

"Is that for me?" She set the limbs on the ground and stood in the doorway.

"Yes. The chief decided he didn't want you weaving or sitting with the women, so he told Hala to see to it you got your own. She'll be bringing wool later."

"I can't go anywhere?" Maggie watched as he laid the pieces down and fit them together.

"To get water and bread, that's what he said."

"Great." Maggie hadn't been alone with Enver since the morning he had given her the carpet to read when he left to get Lahli. She thought of just blurting it out. The chief knows where the sheep are. Why don't we just go and get them? She could prove her story and save her reputation.

Enver stepped back and checked his work. "There." He lingered a moment. "You look better."

"I am. Thanks." She pulled her scarf off and hung it on the loom. "Lahli told me you sacrificed your reputation to the other tribes for me."

Enver lit a cigarette. "She shouldn't have said anything."

"Hala told me that, too."

"She shouldn't have said anything either. This is man's business," Enver said.

It came in a rush. "I'm glad they told me. I don't care what the chief thinks of me, he's only tough around people he can control, but I do care what the women think, and I do care what Lahli thinks, and I care what you think." Maggie inspected the toe of her clog. "I know if it hadn't been for you none of the women would have anything to do with me at all."

Enver propped up against a tree. "I didn't want to bring you here, but I'd have to say now you've proven yourself. I think it's been very hard."

"You could say that." Maggie didn't want to think about it yet. When this was over, if it ever was over, she would never put herself into a situation like this again. Never be where one individual could break her spirit and drain her of her life and health.

He pushed his hair back. "Can you live with this punishment?" he asked.

"Yes. This I can live with," Maggie said.

He lit a cigarette. "You never told anyone about your arm. How is it?"

Maggie extended her arm, pushed up her blouse sleeve to reveal its normal size, without her compression sleeve. "See?"

His eyes narrowed. "So, when you're not working as a nomad you don't have problems?" he asked.

"Occasionally, but not too often." Maggie fleetingly

thought of the drunk man's car and Robert's bat.

Enver ground out the cigarette with the heel of his boot. "I don't like your being out this far away from the tribe." Enver's frown was deep. "I'll talk to the chief."

Maggie bent over the pile of brush and selected a few sprigs to start her fire. "Please don't. Every time someone tries to help me with him it gets worse." She struck a match on a stone and blew on the little pile of wood. "Really."

"If that's what you want." Enver turned and walked toward two grazing camels and passed Hala on her way to Maggie's door.

༻༺

Hala moved slowly, stopping to break off a sprig of something green and sniff it. Maggie waved her inside. "Please come in." This was her second visitor in less than half an hour. "I can't offer you tea." Maggie motioned to the *şamovar* in the corner. "I don't have any."

Hala stuck her hand into an old felt bag she had brought, and pulled out a string of figs, a round of yufka, several slices of dried jerky, one cup of yogurt, some tea leaves, and a handful of pistachios. She handed Maggie the tea. "Now you do."

Maggie moved to blow the small banked fire back to life and added tea leaves and water to the şamovar. She held the two glasses up to the sunlight and wiped them spotless with the cloth used to wrap the bread.

Hala arranged herself on the floor. "I'm going to start your kilim. You can spin and watch."

Maggie twirled the hand spindle. She had learned to let the wool speak to her, to follow the tension of the strands. She would never be a master at the craft, but she prided herself on it being acceptable.

Hala rummaged around in another of her big sacks. She lifted out skein after skein of vibrant indigo, burgundy, cream, black, green, yellow and dark brown wool. She hung the tribal colors, indigo and burgundy, at the top of the loom. It was the long strands of the spring cutting, the best wool. With the motion of untold generations, Hala pointed to the indigo colored wool. "I'll start." Her hands moved in a slow but steady rhythm.

Sunbeams poured through an opening in the goat-haired covering of the hut and danced in wild abandonment on Hala's hands. She sat with her back to the rays, unknowingly in a shaft of light that illuminated only her.

Maggie spun in silence. The fire crackled, the water hissed and somewhere in the distance the faint voice of a shepherd could be heard.

"Why did Mustafa Beyter send you to us?" Hala continued to weave.

Maggie's pulse quickened. She expelled a long breath of air. "To ask you to weave your own histories into the carpets you sell. Let people who really do appreciate them buy them—and they will. He was afraid," Maggie had to get this right, "that you would stop weaving your histories and your ancient tribal language and colors will die." Maggie sat up on her knees and stared straight at Hala. "He went around to many places and bought this tribe's carpets to show the world what you do."

Hala's doubt settled in her face. "He did this?"

"Yes, you can ask Enver or Dr. Lahli or Haluk." Maggie leaned forward. "Mr. Beyter wanted this tribe, you, to never lose your knowledge, and he was afraid it would go away like the histories of the other nomads. But here with you and the women in his tribe he could do something about it." Maggie slowed down her speech. This was too important for anything to be lost in the translation. "He made a lot of money …"

Hala leaned forward, too. "Did he find gold?"

"No, he made a small pump that Enver uses to fix the trucks when he's in the village, or that Lahli can use in her lab in Antalya."

Hala sat back and crossed her arms. "We don't want to owe him. He's dead. We owe nobody."

The enormity of explaining in Turkish exploded in Maggie's head. How could she, one tiny speck of humanity in an endless universe, do this? "Mr. Beyter saved his money like you save carpets to sell at the village. He wanted to use his money to buy your carpets and let you pass them down to your sons and daughters. Or, maybe you would let honest people who would appreciate them buy them at a fair price. They would never forget that women like you know how to speak through your weaving."

"This isn't what the chief says." Hala rubbed her hands together. "He says you want to use Mustafa Beyter's money to control our lives."

Maggie bit the tip of her tongue. She picked at a lingering scab on her arm.

"Stop that." Hala slapped Maggie's hand.

Maggie held her stinging fingers. She had to try one last time. "Mustafa Beyter sent me only because he couldn't come. He told me to tell you that what you do is important and that you need to keep doing it. When we leave the yayla and go down to the village, I'll go back to Antalya, and you, Ashil—all the women—have to decide what to do." Maggie knelt before the old woman. She reached out and covered the weathered hands with her own. In a low voice she didn't recognize the words to fulfill her promise to Mr. Beyter sprang in a torrent from a place deep within her. "Hala, weave the colors of your voice into your proud histories so people like me can look at them and know, there lived a tribe of wise women who knew how to make a loom sing. Tell us why you laughed and why you cried and that you did it in every knot you tied and every row you weaved from every bit of wool you dyed yourselves."

"The colors of our voice," Hala whispered to herself. She closed her eyes and rocked back and forth. She hummed a moment and started singing in a soft voice. Maggie listened, mesmerized by the tale. It was a song of love and hope, a young girl ripe to wed and a shepherd with a flock of hardy sheep. But love was not to be. The lonely girl sat at a loom and tied the black knots of despair when her father promised her to an old wealthy man. Hala's voice dropped lower and her hands began to weave a carpet of air. The girl loved the shepherd and wove in regal blues and stunning reds what she could only tell him in her carpet. He went to war and the girl used plain undyed wool to show her numbed and colorless time. She was wed to the old man, and bore him a son who died before he left the cradle. Maggie wept at the pain in Hala's voice and the sight of her gnarled hands willing her shepherd to come to her. He never came for he had died in the war and the young girl grew old weaving only the black wool of sorrow. Hala folded her hands and bowed her head.

Chapter Sixteen

THE WATER BOILED and Maggie jumped up to make the tea. She busied herself with the glasses, tea, hot water and sugar.

At last Hala opened her eyes. She took the glass from Maggie and sipped quietly. "I'll think about the things you've said."

Finished with her tea, she re-arranged herself in front of the loom. "Move close to me. I'll weave you some eagles because they're strong, and I think you're strong." She worked the wool at a steady pace until a row of eagles in vibrant tribal colors made up the bottom row of Maggie's rug. "Now, I leave you to weave. This kilim belongs to you."

"I don't know where to start, what to weave."

"Start at the beginning." Hala stood up slowly. "Start where the colors take you. I'm tired." She picked up her empty bags and her walking stick. "I'll come back tomorrow."

She meandered down the path toward the camp. She stopped to rub her hips, leaned over and picked a handful of scraggly looking plants and stuffed them into her pocket.

Maggie was famished. She poured tea, spooned yogurt on the bread, wrapped it around two pieces of jerky and ate her supper. She followed it with figs, and cracked some pistachio nuts. Sated, she sat back and stuffed the wool back into the pillow she had destroyed. She dug around in her duffel bag and found a needle and thread. When the breeze shifted she could hear the sounds of the camp and the faint melody of a flute.

She was pouring more tea when she saw Enver and Reza in an almost run coming toward the hut. She stood up and stepped out to meet them. Breathing hard, they came to a halt in front of her.

"Welcome to my home. I'd offer you some tea but I only have two glasses."

"It isn't tea we want." Enver quickly brushed aside the long cultural greetings. "Reza knows where the sheep are, and we're going to get them."

"So do I. They're in a corral at the Urgaz camp." She sat down on a rock near the door. "Please sit down."

Enver squatted down in front of her, the color draining from his face. "How did you know that?"

"I was sitting behind a boulder in the flowers by the edge of the path when Reza told the chief where they were," Maggie said.

Enver motioned Reza down on the ground beside him. "What did the chief say?"

"He told Reza that I let them out and for him not to tell anyone," Maggie said.

Enver looked at Reza and back at Maggie. "That's what Reza said he said." He swore softly.

Maggie waited until the muscle twitching in his cheek

slowed down. "Don't go get them on my account."

Both men frowned at her and stood up.

"I mean it. I don't have anything to prove anymore." Saying it aloud brought an instant relief to Maggie. "Go get them, give the chief the glory, it's all he'll ever get, and leave me out of it."

Enver bent over and pulled her up and stood her in front of him. "What are you saying? This is proof you didn't let them out, and that Saz you saw is probably a shepherd in on this."

"No, he isn't. Stop shaking my arm." Maggie carefully balanced the hot tea glass in both hands before the verbal explosion she had the good sense to anticipate occurred. "That Saz herder is Leslihan's new husband."

"What?" Both men shouted simultaneously. Enver threw his walking stick as far into the air as he could, and it tumbled end over end to fall into the trees. Reza kicked the dirt and then kicked it again.

"Why didn't you *tell* me?" Enver's hands trembled.

"Because you were in Antalya getting Lahli, and then the wedding happened." Somehow it didn't matter anymore. Maggie set the glass down. "Listen to me. The chief wanted me to fail, and he tried to get me to do so, but I didn't. I may not be able to give you Mr. Beyter' s money, but the women still talk to me, they care about me, and that donkey's-ass chief can't take that away." Maggie had never felt more alive, more sure of herself. "Go get the sheep, become heroes and do whatever it is you do to keep that chief of yours in power."

"This isn't right." Enver shook the tree to get his walking

stick down.

"Of course it is. You win, the chief wins, the tribe wins and I win because I've been banished here, to a place I already like, and I don't have to work anymore except to weave my own kilim." Maggie started laughing, she tried to stop, but the irony was too much. She laughed harder, at that pompous chief, unable to stand up to Lahli. Then he had followed Maggie herself around the camp and stoned her—from the back, no less; hiding sheep to make himself look good. He had thought sending her to the hut was the ultimate punishment, but it was where she had finally delivered the message from Mr. Beyter to Hala. Did he know what a great thing he had done for her?

She looked at Reza and Enver and fell into a paroxysm of silent laughter that caused her to hold her sides and gasp, straining to catch a breath. The more the chief punished her, the better she fared!

She wiped the tears from her eyes. The sight of Enver and Reza, stone-faced in the middle of her laughing storm, made her whoop again in helpless peals. She fought in vain to gain some semblance of control over herself. Enver and Reza shrugged to each other and finally chuckled at her self-induced fit of laughter, the cause of which they never knew.

౿

Alone at last, Maggie washed her dish and stored her small cache of food. Enver and Reza had finally left her, puzzled at her behavior, but satisfied she hadn't found a bottle of raki and indulged. She didn't know what they were going to do, and hadn't asked.

She walked around the loom. She had no idea what she wanted to say. Start at the beginning Hala had said. Where was the beginning for her? She unfolded a worn kilim she had found in a corner of the hut, took a long pillow of Ashil's, and bolstered it with two smaller ones on each side. She sat down cross legged to wait.

Throughout the summer she had weaved a few rows on the kilims of the women who had asked her to do so. She had woven a baby's cradle and left her thread, a bright pink one on Tamay's, who had just given birth to beautiful girl. She had woven rows of ram's horns for the abundance of milk from Zeynep's flock of healthy sheep, and left a green thread. For Ashil, she had woven rows of scorpions, to protect her and Ali from harm and left her a white thread of abiding friendship. All of this had been before her fall from grace.

She inspected the row of eagles woven by Hala. Strength. Was there a motif for falling from grace, should she put it in her carpet, and was there one for rising again?

Maggie shivered. A band of clouds had blocked the sun. She pulled her quilt from her duffel bag and wrapped up in it.

The beginning, Hala had said. She ran her hands over the memories of every square. This quilt was a part of her past life. A new life story lay before her and she would weave her own history on a nomad's loom in a hut in the verdant yayla.

Maggie recognized the laughter before she saw Tamay and Zeynep appear at her door. Tamay was loaded with bags, and Zeynep had a bucket of water in each hand.

"We're here to bring you bread and water." Tamay dropped the bags near the log at the door. Zeynep set the buckets down just inside the door.

Maggie was pleased in a way she never expected. "Please, let me put the tea on." She quickly put the water on to boil.

Tamay opened the bags and placed the contents on the old kilim on the ground. A tin of yogurt, a strand of figs, dried cheese and fresh yufka, more tea, honey and olives. "The chief said we could bring you bread and water," her voice muffled deep inside another bag, "but he didn't say we couldn't bring you anything else."

Maggie enjoyed the sight of the feast before her; enough for several days, even if she shared it with six others. "I hope you're hungry."

Zeynep rubbed her face. "Always."

Maggie went to get the tea. She would serve her guests in the two glasses she had, and let them eat together off her single plate.

"May I weave a row on your kilim?" Tamay sat down in a graceful sweep.

"I'd be honored," Maggie said. "Anything you want." She didn't have a tray, but Maggie had found a thin slab of wood when she first arrived. It had probably been used by the shepherds and herders as a serving tray. She wiped it off and arranged the glasses on it.

Stone the Goat

Zeynep joined Tamay at the loom. They told Maggie of the daily goings-on in the camp, sipped their tea, shared olives and bread, and busied their hands with fine wool. They stayed until Tamay stood up and stretched.

"We have to go, Hala wants us to make bread, and Sema has been watching the baby," Tamay said.

Zeynep poured water into Maggie's stoneware pitchers, and slipped the empty buckets on her arm. "Do you need anything?"

"Yes. Please bring me some orange and pink wool."

"You're not getting married or having a baby," Tamay laughed, "why do you want orange and pink wool?"

"No, but I need those colors. You'll see why when I'm finished." This was Maggie's kilim, and it didn't have to meet the nomad tradition. She felt bold, and a bold rug she would weave.

When the women had said their goodbyes and Maggie could no longer hear their voices, she stooped down to see what each had woven into her rug.

Tamay had used the tribal indigo and added white to make a motif of an eye used to repel evil. She had left a long white strand of wool. Zeynep had woven a row of phoenix on the tribe's burgundy background, brown birds that die only to rise again. She had left a burgundy strand.

Maggie gathered up the piles of wool. She picked out a skein of brightest yellow and one of robin egg blue. She would weave carnations. These rows would be her mother, the sunshine and blue sky of her life. Then Maggie selected a rich brown, for the memory of her father's weathered hands. She would weave a bird, for he had taken flight, and somewhere in that row she would weave a strand of black, for her despair when he had left without a word.

Maggie sat down in front of the loom and laid her face against the soft wool. She reached for the blue and yellow. Slowly at first, gaining confidence row after row, Maggie gained control of the history of her life.

Ashil visited daily, and wove Ali's family motif, two triangles, and the rams' horn for an abundant life for Maggie. She left a telltale thread of green for a growing friendship.

Enver checked on her daily. He brought water and wood, unexpected but appreciated. Maggie would have loved to ask him about the English woman he had brought to the village years ago, the one who left after one week. Maggie wanted to say, see, I did it, I stayed. She said nothing instead.

In the weeks remaining Maggie worked swiftly to finish her kilim. Hala, Ashil, Tamay, Sema and many of the women came often and sustained her with food, water and friendship. They laughed and shook their heads in disbelief at the colors Maggie was weaving into her rug.

She had paired black with orange, the Oklahoma State University school colors, which Robert had waved and worn with love for his alma mater. He had always sat next to Mr. Beyter at the sporting events, who had gently waved the school colors of the institution, wearing a muted orange shirt of his own. The last color Maggie used was a vibrant baby blue amid some black for the son she never bore Robert. She finished her kilim on the day before autumn swept down the yayla.

The wind had changed. Maggie lay on her sleeping carpets and heard it in the leaves on the trees. There was a bite to the morning air. She dug around in her bag and found her calendar. Soon. They would be leaving the yayla soon.

༄

Maggie stood by the truck door. She looked at the rows of trucks, the piles and bundles, the children zooming around in last minute expulsions of energy. She wasn't riding in the lead truck today. Enver and the chief were together for the return trip.

"Ready to go?" Ashil stepped around the rear of the truck. She sighed deeply. "I'm never ready to leave."

"Not even when the snow starts?" Maggie teased.

"Oh, yes, when the snow comes," Ashil smiled. "If it could just stay as it is …"

Maggie laughed. "Know what you mean. There are some moments that just shouldn't end," she put her arm around Ashil, "but this one should—for me anyway."

"I know what your moment is," Ashil said. "You are dreaming of wearing a scarf, hunting for plants for the dyes and making yufka."

They both laughed at that.

They could see Ali coming from the lead truck. When he arrived, he walked around the truck and looked at it carefully. Satisfied with what he saw, he said, "We're ready now. Let's go down the mountain."

Maggie was glad to be riding with Ashil and Ali. Now that they were actually on their way, she could believe it was over.

Over. She breathed deeply. It's all over but the shoutin'. Hooty Tooty Hannah, had all I can standah. Gimme a big O, a big V, a big E, a big R! ...

No one had said a word about the chief accepting the Beyter Foundation offer to buy any and all of the familial carpets the women might weave. In a moment she would never forget, Maggie had verbalized Mr. Beyter's desire in a way that Hala had understood. She could do no more.

Ahead was civilization, her fabulous suite, that crazy Haluk, and Lahli. All that was left was to get to the village.

Maggie looked backward out the window at the grazing grounds and to the mountains beyond. She mouthed a silent goodbye to the yayla.

*

Maggie piled the two duffel bags in the corner of her room in Ashil's house. It seemed a palace after the trek to the yayla. She left her toothbrush and pajamas on the table and gazed wistfully around the room. This would be her last night in the company of nomads.

The trip down had been easier than the trip up. Perhaps it was because she knew what to expect, or that she was getting closer to going home. Tomorrow she would leave the village for Antalya.

"Are you doing fine?" Tamay asked her on her way to Hala's. "You look far away."

"Yes, I am," Maggie said as she picked up a water bucket. "I'm going to miss this place, these people," she continued, mostly to herself.

They had arrived the day before, and the massive unpacking and placement of goats, including the missing herd that had miraculously been found by the chief, had begun.

She heard the chickens squawk, and saw Enver coming. Ashil had gone to Hala's with fresh yogurt, and Ali was helping corral the last of the flocks of sheep.

She didn't wait for him to call her. She had seen him often during her banishment; not on the trip from the yayla. He had spent more of his time with the chief, Ashil had said.

She opened the door and stepped onto the porch. Branches on the olive tree that shaded the hen house sagged with dark plump bounty. The tree near the porch was speckled with the toast colored shells of ripe almonds, it's leaves rustling slightly in the breeze. The scent and sound of autumn hung heavy in the air.

Enver slung his camel saddle from his shoulder and dropped a bundle of fresh straw for the hen house at his feet. "I've come to say goodbye. I wanted to tell you myself I won't be taking you to Antalya tomorrow."

Maggie sucked in her breath. She had counted on it, had dreamt about it. This time would be different. He was going to talk to her. She could tease him about losing the bet to put goats in Haluk's condo, find out how long he would be staying in Antalya, have dinner with him, tell him a proper goodbye.

"Ali and Reza are going to collect the indigo plants near the ocean and I need to stay and repair some fence." He looked as if he needed to be elsewhere at that moment. "They'll take good care of you."

Maggie stopped breathing. She felt the evening breeze on her face. A full moon rested between two peaks of the silhouetted mountains. She spoke very low, "You asked me in the yayla if I would kiss you, before you went to get Lahli. Do you remember that?"

"Yes," Enver said.

"Do you still want to?" Maggie held her breath.

He took a half step closer and stopped. His eyes bored into her. He reached down and picked up the saddle in one hand.

Say something.

"You told me Hala told you to keep your smell," he said in a voice with a pain she could feel. He picked up the straw bundle in the other hand.

Maggie's throat closed as the barriers between them mounted. She picked up the largest water jug on the step and held it tightly to her chest. "She did."

"She was right," he said.

Maggie could only nod. Still tightly clasping the heavy water pot, she turned and went up the steps to the door. She bit her cheek then turned around and said in a clear voice. "Goodbye, Enver."

His voice was ragged, his English perfect. "Goodbye, Maggie. A nomad woman of the Urek tribe."

Stone the Goat

Her eyes followed him as he walked, back to the village, to his people, his life; the night shielding him from view. She stepped inside the house and gently set the water pot down. She leaned her head against the door jamb and slid down the wall.

You wanted his respect, you got it.

Chapter Seventeen

THE SOUNDS AND the smells of the city assaulted her—diesel fuel, smoke, honking, milling pedestrians, cars, cabs, store front windows reflecting the sun, endless streams of humanity on their way to office buildings and time constraints.

"We have you there, almost." Ali smiled broadly. He had been entrusted to get her to the Residence Hotel, and he made the last left turn off the boulevard to drive carefully down the impossible streets of Old Town.

"Much safer than when Haluk brings me," Maggie returned his smile. She was eager to arrive at the hotel, ready for her old life, which she knew would never be the same. Some part of her had remained amid the carpeted tents of the Urek tribe.

Kemal, the proprietor of the hotel was standing in the doorway when the truck came to a gentle stop. Omar, the carpet merchant waved from his shop next door.

A well-dressed doorman stepped out, opened the door for Maggie and handed her off to Kemal.

The portly man beamed. "Welcome back, Maggie Hanim. You survived the yayla."

"About those letters I was going to write …"

"Ah, yes. I heard the carrier pigeons took a holiday to Cyprus and were not available to deliver your letters, is that what you heard?"

"Something like that." Maggie held out both hands to the rotund man. "It's good to be back. I hope you have room for me. I had no way to contact you."

"Haluk arranged everything. You have the same suite, and," he walked around the spotless counter, "also, a letter has just arrived for you." Kemal handed Maggie the heavy brass key and a crisp white envelope.

In a dreamlike trance, Maggie walked up the marble staircase, turned the key and opened the door. The French windows were slightly ajar, a bouquet of exquisite roses held court on the desk, and an autumn breeze tickled the white curtains. She dropped her bags on the floor and fell face forward into the soft thick down of the comforter. With a whish it billowed around her and fell downward, to cover her in warmth.

Maggie closed her eyes. She stretched out as far as her toes could reach, then rolled to the left, back to the right, turned on her back and stretched again.

It would take time, but she would get past Enver. She wasn't the first woman to succumb to a handsome man in an exotic location. Two of her friends had fallen in love and married the men they had met in foreign countries. One was happy, the other miserable.

The phone jangled. She raised her head to look at it and then laughed aloud. She didn't have to answer it! She burrowed her head into the comforter, drank in the smell of fresh linens and soap, listened to the faint sound of a motor on a boat in the harbor and realized she was ravenous.

The phone rang again. "What?" Maggie growled into the receiver.

"Dinner at eight; drinks in the lounge at seven, wear something that shows your legs and arms and a dash of lipstick would be good too." Haluk's voice filled her ear.

"Still telling me what to do?" Maggie smiled into the phone. "You haven't spent six months in a tent, eating from a tray on the ground, and you want to see me at seven all gussied up?" Maggie rolled over and lifted her left leg straight into the air. "Surely you don't mean today, because I intend to stay in that shower ..."

"Until I come and drag you out? I will you know." Haluk's voice deepened. "Be here at seven, looking good, and prepared to eat and drink with me until the wee hours of the morning. Then, I'll escort you to your room, and this time you can ask me to stay. Or, I'll sadly be off."

"If I wake up, I'll be there. No promises today," Maggie said.

"Seven it is then. Don't be late."

Maggie laid the phone carefully on its base and with her arm still outstretched, was asleep in an instant.

༄

"Are you happy to be back?" Haluk sipped the demitasse of Turkish coffee. "You've changed, you know. I've been waiting for a long time, maybe half an hour."

"Just getting even for all those years I sat around waiting on you." Maggie had leisurely managed to arrive in the lounge at half past seven. "Besides, with hot steamy showers, big thick towels, a hair dryer, a staff at my beck and call, wouldn't you be happy to be back, and possibly late?"

"I would never have gone, actually. I would have honored Mr. Beyter in some other fashion."

"No choice for me. I'm glad I went, but I didn't accomplish what Mr. Beyter wanted." Maggie shook her head.

"I hear that you did."

"You're kidding," Maggie said.

"No, Enver told me," Haluk said.

"Oh, yes. Enver, your brother, *that* Enver," Maggie shook her head at him.

"Sorry. I should have told you before you left, but I knew you would never go with him if you knew he was my brother." Haluk plucked at the tablecloth.

"Why do you say that?" Maggie asked.

"You couldn't stand me watching over you, and Mr. Beyter made it clear that was my job." Haluk ran his fingers through his hair. "Going off with my brother was just an extension of me, and you would have gone out and found some unsavory man, and maybe we would never have seen you again." Haluk leaned forward. "I didn't want anything to happen to you."

With the clarity of hindsight Maggie had to agree.

"Did you learn to read the carpets?" Haluk asked.

"Yes. I did." Maggie smiled at the memory of Hala bent over an ancient carpet, singing it aloud in a lullaby voice.

"Did you teach the women how to negotiate for a good price at the markets?"

"All I did was tell them about westerners and how foreign bartering is to them. I told them to stand firm in their prices. Haluk, I got them to role play." Maggie got tickled telling the tale, "You should have seen Sema playing a fat man using her finger as a moustache! It was too funny."

Maggie motioned to a waiter for more coffee. The sweet Turkish coffee warmed its way down her throat and flooded her with its flavor. "I discovered something. Those women are masters at negotiation. I watched them with their husbands." Maggie laughed softly, "They know how to work those men."

"Women everywhere know how to get us to do what they want." Haluk sat back and crossed his legs.

Maggie coughed discreetly into her napkin, nodding. "Of course, we do. That's why we rule the world and all the men work for us."

"So, now what?" Haluk asked. "What's next after this big adventure? A long vacation, I hope. I've been thinking …"

"You know, Kemal gave me a letter when I checked in, and I forgot about it." Maggie reached for her purse and rifled through it. "Here." She opened the envelope from the headquarters office of the Beyter Foundation in London and scanned its contents.

"And?" Haluk tapped a foot.

"I've been asked to report to London in four weeks to prepare for a project in …" she flipped to the second page.

"In?" Haluk was impatient.

"India, just east of Goa, an orphanage needs some help." Maggie dropped the letter on the table. "I've been in Turkey off and on for seven years. It makes sense to go somewhere else for a while, doesn't it?"

"No. There's a lot to do here, and you can speak our language," Haluk said.

"Not as well as I'd like. I needed nomad Turkish in the yayla."

"Well enough to call the chief a donkey's ass," Haluk said.

"How did you know I said that?" Maggie asked.

"The chief told Enver, and he told me. That's very brave, Maggie, and very funny." Haluk's face broke into a megawatt grin. "He is an ass. I couldn't stay there for even one week. I don't know how Enver does it."

Maggie twisted her napkin into a tight wad. "It's the life he wants. He certainly doesn't belong here."

"Enver doesn't belong there, either." Haluk shot back. "The only reason they have anything modern is because he has begged and pleaded with them. I'd leave them alone."

Maggie untwisted the napkin, spread it out on the table, and ran her fingers over the deep wrinkles. "He doesn't fit in either place."

"Where do you fit?" Haluk asked.

"I don't fit anywhere either, just a different sort of nomad."

"Speaking of nomads," Haluk looked over Maggie's shoulder and spoke to someone she couldn't see. "You should see this one. Join us for a drink?"

Maggie caught a whiff of almond soap. She was afraid to

turn around. She had allowed her loneliness and isolation to mistake Enver's kindness during her banishment as something more.

"Yes. I'll buy the raki." Enver signaled a waiter and ordered, slid a chair around the table and sat down next to Haluk. "I see you made it back," he smiled slightly at Maggie, "Good thing it wasn't Haluk driving you."

Once again Maggie was speechless at the contrast in Enver. He shrugged out of a cinnamon silk jacket, slid a brown envelope out of a pocket and handed it to Maggie. "For you."

"Yes, it's a good thing your *brother* Haluk didn't drive me. He'd have stopped for a camel race somewhere." Maggie smiled back, accepting the envelope.

The drinks arrived. Haluk stood and lifted his glass to Maggie. "A toast," he bent over in an exaggerated bow. "To our newest Urek nomad. Thanks to you I am goat and donkeyless in my condo—which Enver would absolutely have brought with him if you hadn't stayed six months."

"Isolation helped," Maggie said. "But not enough to get the chief to take Mr. Beyter's money. I tried. I really did." She inspected the envelope. "What's this?" She looked back and forth between Enver and Haluk. "What is it?"

"Open it and read it aloud, if you want to." Enver opened his gold cigarette case.

Maggie unfolded a single page. It was written in stilted Turkish, and there were two ink spots near the end. She glanced quickly at the signature—Abdul, the chief.

Mary Walley Kalbert

Maggie Hanim,

The Urek tribe of Anatolia agrees to accept the money from Mustafa Beyter, whose mother was a member of our tribe. She lived and died among us. Our women will preserve our ways of weaving carpets and our history will be passed on to our children, and our children's children. The world will know our women are the best weavers in all of Anatolia.

Maggie re-read the letter. "He didn't write this. What's going on? How did this happen?"

Enver fiddled with a cigarette between his fingers. "Hala told the women that they needed to weave their histories in the colors of their voices so people could look at them and say, those are wise women who know how to make a loom sing, and how to make a carpet laugh or cry in every knot they tie and every row they weave." He picked up his raki glass and looked at Maggie. "I never knew our Hala was so eloquent. The women told their husbands the same thing—that they didn't want to use bad wool and make ugly carpets with colors they would never use. They wanted to be remembered as bold women with strong colors who said whatever they wanted to say in their carpets. Then the men discussed it and you know the rest."

"Why wouldn't the chief tell me this before I left the village? Maggie asked.

"To save face," Enver and Haluk said simultaneously.

Maggie looked deep into the milky liquor and saw the wrinkle lined face of Hala weaving carpets in the air. She raised her glass and smiled at both men, "Good for Hala. She should be your chief."

A quiet peace flowed through Maggie. Mr. Beyter had been right. Change did happen in the time and the rhythm of the nomads. And change was happening to her.

Enver lit his cigarette. "Now what for you?"

"I've been offered a job in Goa. I might take it. First, I have a stop to make in London at the foundation and then I'm going back to a ranch in Oklahoma." *And back to an old battered lunchbox...* She paused a moment. "It's kind of like the yayla, a place where my husband's tribe gets together."

There are shepherds for cattle, Maggie thought, and generations of kids to teach about life on a ranch. She was still a part of that family if she wished to be.

"Here's what I think," Haluk interjected. "Tell the foundation to forget Goa. Tell them you'll manage their Turkish affairs from the Residence Hotel and you need a new car every year..."

"Let me guess, from you." Maggie stopped him.

"Sure, why not me?" Haluk looked puzzled.

Enver ignored Haluk. He blew smoke out the side of his mouth, and away from Maggie's direction. "I might see you in London, need to go there a few days myself." He finished his raki and stood up to leave.

Maggie didn't stand. She held out her hand for him to shake. He bent and kissed it instead. Her pulse quickened. Her voice was strong. "Goodbye, Enver." For the first time since she had met him Maggie held the power. It would never work between them. The flame would spark, then fizzle out and die among the stones in the yayla. She would become the bride, Enver's property, and the entire tribe would be the mother-in-law she could never please. She looked him full in the face without hiding the bittersweet emotion she knew was evident there.

Maggie pulled her hand back gently. "Go with God", she said in English.

"Goodbye," Enver said, releasing her hand. He nodded goodbye to Haluk, picked up his jacket and walked away.

Maggie watched him for a moment then turned her attention to Haluk. "Stay here and buy a car from you, is that what you said?" She lifted her glass of raki in a toast, "to you and your crazy ideas, *Şerefe*."

❧

Maggie sat in the lobby of the hotel, her two duffel bags stacked neatly against the wall. She had tried to get a cab to the airport, but the uproar from Kemal and Haluk overpowered her. Haluk would eventually arrive and get her there on time. He always did. One day he would cut it a little tight and she would miss her plane. If it happened today, she wouldn't kill, but might possibly maim him.

It had taken three days and three sleepless nights to assimilate back into city life.

She and Lahli had driven the short distance to Aspendos and Perge to walk among the Roman ruins. They had bought kebabs and eaten them in front of the statue of Apollo in the

Stone the Goat

seaside town of Side. Lahli agreed she should spend as long as she wanted in Oklahoma. They agreed to meet in Barcelona before Maggie headed to Goa.

Maggie recognized the gentle hum of a car that purred its way to a stop in front of the hotel. Haluk had arrived. She should get her things together. She heard footsteps on the marble floor. In a moment Haluk stood in front of her chair. "I don't believe it. You're knitting."

"Yes, I am." Maggie's hand clicked steadily to the end of a row. She held up a separate well-formed sock.

"Is it a courting sock? Is it for me?" Haluk's pleasure in her probable answer was palpable.

"No, it is not. It's a friendship sock. A new tradition," she looked at him over the needles, "Still want it?"

He sighed. "I don't suppose a courting sock would be following at a later date?"

"Nope."

Haluk bent over to admire the dark blue and tan colors. He ran his hands over the fine spring wool, dyed deep indigo and inspected the dark sand colored border. "A friendship sock?" He gently ruffled Maggie's hair. "I'll take it. Better to have a sock you like than not have one at all."

Maggie smiled, dropped the knitting into her bag and snapped it shut. "I agree."

Acknowledgements

In the beginning and the end: Pam, Mike and Kathleen.
In the fledgling stage: Holly, Susan, Marc and Tony.
In the first full draft: Alice, Lindsey, Claudia, Lindsay, Sherryl, Kare, Rachel, Lori and Laura.
All drafts after: Carol, Mary, Cyndi, Cheryl, Walter and Pat.
Alice B. Acheson for years of advice which have never failed me.
Donald Maass for a writing workshop that made me mad, resentful, hopeless, blank-minded, sulky, reflective, thoughtful, determined, excited, and finally finished, having accomplished my personal best.
To all others whom I have acknowledged privately and sincerely, you know who you are.

Mary Walley Kalbert is the author of *Reflections on Life in the San Juan Islands*. She is a World War II memoirist and former columnist for islandguardian.com. She enjoys photography and cooking. Mary and her husband enjoy traveling. They share their home in the San Juan Islands with one contented cat.

Visit Mary at www.marywalleykalbert.com

Questions for Discussion

1. Does the protagonist, Maggie Meadows resonate with you? Can you relate to her losses? If so, how? Do they define her?

2. Does the setting become a 'character' in this novel? Is it a vital part of this novel, a force to be reckoned with? How does the setting affect Maggie?

3. In how many ways is Maggie's character conflicted? Is there inner and outer conflict? Are the nomad women conflicted by Maggie's choices? When? Why?

4. What is at stake for Maggie? Is it greater than fulfilling a promise to Mr. Beyter? Are there personal stakes involved as well?

5. Does Maggie's journey transform her? Is it possible Mr. Beyter had a two-fold reason to send Maggie on this journey? In addition to her promise to him, was he giving her this opportunity to come to terms with her past and make peace with herself?